13

VOLUME 1

LINDLEY VALCARCEL

Edited by
A. B. ALVAREZ

UNLIKELY EXPERIMENTS

For
Kara and Aphra

CONTENTS

FRIENDLY CHAT, PART 1

I talk to my dead girlfriend. My therapist suggested it as a form of healing or acceptance or maybe just because she thought I don't tell her enough of what's on my mind and she thinks I need the practice.

At first I thought the exercise was pretty useless. I'm not the kind of person that talks to myself out loud, much less to someone who is dead. I tried starting by just thinking what I wanted to say in my head. But that was somehow worse. My therapist said that was because I was getting too stuck in my head. I needed to talk things out.

I decided to start small. I was getting ready for class and grabbed my phone. I had meant to send Jaime a text but then the gut punch of remembering she was gone hit me. I gripped the phone so tightly my knuckles went white.

"I miss you," I said quietly to the empty air of my dorm room. I couldn't get anything else out before the lump in my throat shut down any thought I had of continuing. I got up and went to class.

Two days later I put a bunch of food from the dining hall into a to-go box and went to eat it in my room. "They had your favorite today." I poked at the goopy mac and cheese that Jaime had always enjoyed. I couldn't figure out why, it was literally just large quantities of the boring boxed stuff. But it made me feel better having some. I squeezed my eyes closed and for a moment I imagined I could feel her hand on my shoulder. Without thinking I moved a hand to my shoulder but the sensation disappeared. I sighed and ate the cold mac and cheese.

I slowly started to talk more to Jaime over time. It was easier after about a week. Especially as my other living friends skirted around me whenever I saw them in class. They were friendly enough, sure, but they always vanished quickly. Sometimes I felt like they thought Jaime's ghost was hanging around me or something the way they looked spooked and would dart away quickly if they could.

I tried to only talk to her when I was in my room and I was alone. I told her stupid stuff, all the little things I would normally have texted her or told her when I knew she was in a bad mood. I read her some stupid joke I found online and looked up, automatically expecting to see her sitting there rolling her eyes at me.

"You're an idiot, Jenna."

I blinked. Even though I knew what I would see I scanned my dorm room. It was empty. But I could have sworn I heard Jaime's voice. My stomach sank. Great, now I was imagining things. My therapist was going to have a field day with that.

"It isn't uncommon for people to see the people they cared about after they've died," was all she told me when I mentioned it. "She's living within you. Within your memories."

That thought bounced around in my head for days. I kept talking to Jaime. Sometimes I imagined I could smell the detergent she used to clean her clothes. Or hear her laugh after I read a stupid joke. One time I woke up and could have sworn I felt her get out of the bed before my alarm went off. Talking to her felt natural now.

Jaime had been dead for two months when I first saw her. I was on my way to one of my evening classes, the one she used to wait for me outside of so she could say goodnight. My heart skipped a beat and I ground to a halt.

"Jaime!"

As she started to turn someone walked in front of me. I blinked and no one was standing where I'd seen her. A few of the nearby students looked at me but no one stopped or seemed concerned that I'd just called out my dead girlfriend's name. I hunched my shoulders and ignored the pricking feeling in my eyes as I went to class.

This time I didn't tell my therapist what happened. I tried to talk about Jaime as little as possible. She asked but I changed the subject. I talked about my classes, or how my friends had stopped inviting me to things. Especially the ones who had known Jaime as well.

"How do you feel about that? Are you making new friends?"

I hesitated. "It's fine. I'd rather focus on my classes."

That night as I lay in bed I spoke to Jaime as usual. It had become my ritual. I couldn't fall asleep until I'd said at least a few things to her.

"I have that test tomorrow in bio. Think I'll skip my first class tomorrow and try to study for that instead. I miss you reading the notecards for me. I miss…" I trailed off. That damn lump was back in my throat and I squeezed my eyes closed.

"You'll do fine, Jenna."

I didn't open my eyes but I curled up a little tighter in bed. "I miss you."

"I miss you too. Don't skip class. Promise me."

I swallowed hard. It was the one class we'd shared together. I'd barely gone since she died. "I don't want to."

"Please? I can see you better there."

I should have been more worried that I was hallucinating but I couldn't care. I just wanted to hear her voice. "Ok." I told myself not to open my eyes but I did anyway. There was some light coming through my pathetic excuse for curtains and it was enough to make out the shapes of a few things in my room. Out of the corner of my eye I could see someone sitting in my bean bag chair. I wanted to look at her more directly, I wanted to be sure it was her. But I had the feeling if I looked too hard she'd disappear.

"Go to sleep."

I wanted to tell her I was hallucinating but that seemed a bit redundant. A hallucination didn't need to be told what it was. And I welcomed this one. "Night, Jaime," I said and closed my eyes.

"Night, Jenna."

I stopped seeing my therapist after our next session. Partially because I didn't want to tell her about my hallucinations. Partially because my college only gave students ten free therapy sessions a semester.

I kept talking to Jaime. She didn't always talk back but sometimes she did. She started talking back more often than not. As I neared the end of the semester I worried about leaving campus. This was where Jaime and I had spent most of our time together when she'd been alive. This was where she died.

"I want to stay over winter break." It was night and I'd given up studying. It was a good night. Jaime was more talkative than usual.

"Why? Don't you want to go home?"

"Why would I? So my parents can fuss over me? So people I don't care about can act sorry for me?" I didn't say what I was really thinking.

"You can't live here, Jen."

I risked a glance at the bean bag chair. I could see Jaime sitting there but she seemed not quite solid. And if I focused on her too long she'd start to fade. So I kept it to quick glances or I'd stare at a spot near the chair so I could see her out of the corner of my eye. "I can't talk to you at home."

"I'm not going anywhere. Whether you talk to me or not."

I thought about that for a moment. "But you're a hallucination. If I stop talking to you…"

Jaime laughed slightly. "You're an idiot. You're not hallucinating."

"That's what a hallucination would say."

"I'm not in your head. I've been here the whole time. Watching, waiting. For weeks I didn't think you could see me."

I didn't say anything right away. "So you're haunting me?"

"Yes. No. I don't know. I mean… I'm dead. I guess that's what you'd call it then."

"You know I don't believe in ghosts."

"Apparently you don't have to. Because here I am."

I closed my eyes. When I opened them a long moment later Jaime was still sitting in my bean bag chair. "Will you come home with me?"

"Of course. I'm always with you."

That probably should have scared me. Or made me nervous. Or worried for my sanity. But it didn't. Instead I closed my eyes and fell asleep and for the first time in months I was confident that in the morning Jaime would be there for me.

I followed Kate through the crowded streets. I could see that she was a little lost and she consulted the map she'd brought.

"You should've gotten the data plan so you could have a better map," I told her.

Kate squinted at the map and sighed. "I should've gotten the data plan."

I smiled faintly and followed her as she continued down the street. She'd never been to Mexico before. She didn't even speak Spanish. I admired her for coming anyway. Even if I wasn't so sure why she insisted on coming.

Especially as she started going to different stores and picking things out. These weren't souvenirs, or at least not the usual kind. Which made sense; this wasn't exactly a popular tourist location.

It was actually the area that a lot of my family was from.

"I'm still kind of surprised you came." I was looking at the shelf of candy in the store. I was familiar with all of them but I had gotten distracted by some of the other candies they had. There were numerous brightly colored skulls and animals as well as flowers and a few other things. I was so distracted by looking at everything that I didn't realize that Kate had wandered off.

I caught up with her as she left the store. As I fell into step next to her I caught sight of her expression.

She was blinking back tears and seemed to be clutching the bag of candy and pastries for all she was worth. I looked away and didn't say anything.

Later I followed Kate as she wandered the streets some more. She was no longer interested in the shops and the decorations. She had her colorful plastic bag, traditional here in Mexico, filled to the brim with decorations and food. We always had a ton of those bags in my house growing up.

I was enjoying the quiet tour of the town. Kate still seemed distant. I hadn't really seen that look before on her face but I didn't worry. She could handle herself.

As it got later in the day Kate pulled her map out again.

"Aren't you getting hungry?"

Kate sighed and turned the map all around like that would actually help her orient herself. "Ok, this place shouldn't be too far." She started off and I hurried after her.

"I'm not really sure how this works," Kate said softly.

I eyed her but didn't know how to help.

"I mean, I read about it, sure, but that doesn't mean much. I hope I'm doing it right."

"It's going to be fine."

Kate turned down a side street. There were people here, more people than I'd been expecting. I couldn't figure out why until I realized where she was going.

"Oh, Kate…"

The cemetery was surprisingly large for such a small town. The graves were all beautifully decorated with flowers and candles. I saw that each one had some of those colorful candies I'd been admiring in the shop.

Kate stopped to look around and then headed towards one corner of the graveyard. There were no graves or markers in that area.

"I know you're not here," Kate started but kept her voice low like she didn't want to interrupt the other people at the cemetery. Some were still putting up decorations while others were sitting by the graves and chatting quietly, either to the tombstones or to others that were with them. "But I thought it was the most appropriate place to do this."

As I followed Kate she started rummaging through another bag that I hadn't paid any attention to. I'd assumed she'd just been using it as her regular purse. It was certainly large enough for it. Kate had never gotten over the gigantic purse trend that had been so popular not long ago.

She knelt in one corner of the cemetery and started pulling things out of the purse. First was a framed picture of the two of us.

"I can't believe you chose that one," I told her, cringing slightly. It wasn't my favorite of me as it was taken when I hadn't been expecting it. Partially because my face was covered in frosting after she'd smashed some birthday cake on it and I looked stunned. To one side Kate was laughing. My favorite kind of laugh, though, where her head was thrown back and her whole face scrunched up with glee.

"I know it's not your favorite," Kate said as she continued to go through the bag. "But I like it." She pulled a few more things out. A small plushie of our college mascot, a couple of cheap souvenirs from the places we'd gone on our school breaks. Exotic places like the local mini golf place, a keychain from New York City, and a few ticket stubs from movies we'd gone to.

I looked around the graveyard and it suddenly occurred to me what Kate was doing.

"Dia de los muertos," I whispered. I should have known.

She wiped at her eyes and started putting out the candy and the pan de muerto she'd purchased earlier. "Sorry, Rosa, I'm not sure if I'm doing this right."

As she knelt next to the picture frame she adjusted all the items that she'd set out and finally finished the whole thing off with a few small flowers. She just stared at everything for a moment and then started to cry.

I settled next to her, painfully aware of how insubstantial I was. "It's beautiful."

"It's November 1st. I read that it's when…" She trailed off and I ached to be able to comfort her somehow.

"All Souls Day. Adult spirits visit."

"It must seem stupid. I don't really believe that… But you talked so much about your family here." Kate absently adjusted one of the flowers, wiping at her eyes with her other hand. "I thought it would be nice."

"I wanted to bring you here so badly." It wasn't fair she had to make the trip by herself. Without thinking I tried resting one hand on top of hers.

She straightened a little and breathed deeply. "I hated that stupid coconut shampoo when you first started using it."

I smiled a little. "I know."

"I miss you."

"I know that too." I didn't say that I missed her too. Instead I rested my head on her shoulder the way I used to. I didn't think she'd notice but she shivered slightly.

"Rosa?"

"I'm here."

Kate didn't say anything else but I could tell she relaxed. After a minute she started talking. Not about anything in particular. Some of it was recounting a few of the things we'd done together, some was just a general update about what had happened since I'd died. I listened and wondered if she knew I was there.

As it got dark the cemetery started to empty. Reluctantly Kate started to move. She picked up the picture frame and lightly kissed it. Then she got to her feet. I wanted to follow her but I knew I couldn't. All Souls Day was almost over.

"You're going to be ok," I told her.

Kate let out a slow breath and wiped the last tears from her eyes. I could see she was doing her best to keep her composure. "Love you, Rosa. Don't worry, I'll be ok."

I smiled a little and watched her go. I knew that she was right about that much.

MISSING PROMISES

I didn't realize they still made missing person fliers until I started to see the ones with my cousin's face go up in my neighborhood. I passed them regularly and wondered how many people even paid any attention to them anymore. They'd been up for almost three months.

One of the few places I went to regularly where I didn't see the fliers was my job. It was a convenience store on the other side of the highway from where most of my family lived. I'd only been working there for about a month and it was meant to be my summer job before starting college in the fall. I'd agreed to take the 12-hour night shift because I wanted something quiet. Somewhere to get away from the chaos that was tearing my family apart.

The first week was easy enough. I had one other person working with me for training purposes although I was told I'd be on my own once training was complete. We got deliveries during the shift and a handful of customers and not a lot else. I was shown how to work basic security measures. The door locked after midnight and when customers came to the door I had to press a button behind the desk to open it for them. There were a few cameras. One on the parking lot, one inside that recorded anyone coming inside and one on the back door where we received deliveries.

By the end of the first week I felt comfortable with the procedures. I'd set myself up with a book and some quiet music and a list of everything I had to get done in the store that night.

That was the first night I thought my job was a little weird. At exactly midnight I walked into the back to restock and organize the cooler with the drinks. It was the kind where it had to be loaded from the back because the door was in the front where customers could open it and take what they wanted. No one had restocked the drinks in a few hours, since the evening commute rush, and I knew I had a lot to do. I put my earbuds in one ear so I could hear if anyone buzzed at the door to come in and got to work. I hummed along to my music and focused on the stocking.

When I was done I went back behind the counter. It was only eight minutes later from when I went into the back. I stared at the clock in disbelief and confirmed it with my phone clock.

I could have sworn I listened to more than three or four songs while I was stocking. At that point I got distracted from thinking about it as a customer showed up and buzzed the doorbell to be let in. By the time I'd gotten home I'd completely forgotten about it.

I had the next few days off. I spent it with my aunt handing out more fliers and knocking on doors to see if anyone had seen my cousin.

My next shift I got bored so I made a list of things I could do to clean up the store. I was halfway through mopping the entire place when I looked up to check my progress. There were streaks on the floor and I frowned. As I stepped over to take a closer look I saw the shape of footprints.

My heart jumped into my throat and I backed up so quickly I tripped over the mop bucket. Water splashed everywhere and I scrambled back to my feet, holding the mop handle like a weapon.

"Who's there?" I demanded. My voice was shaking just as badly as the rest of me. No one should have been in the store except for me. I hadn't heard the buzzer and the door was locked after midnight. There wasn't any other way in.

I scrambled for what I should do. The water that had splashed out of the bucket had washed some of the prints away. As I examined them I noticed they didn't seem to go in any particular direction but I followed them towards the back office. They simply disappeared there. I looked around the office with my mop handle held in front of me like a protective staff. Once I'd checked the entire store I headed back to the counter. I wasn't sure what to do. If I called the police I'd have to explain the situation to my manager. I hadn't found anyone and the doors were all still locked. Plus the prints were now mixed with my own or the floor had dried and they were gone now.

I decided to simply clean up and forget it. I had probably just back-tracked and forgotten about it. I'd be more careful the next time I mopped the floor.

One of the few things that had annoyed me about the job from the start were the security cameras. There weren't many but they seemed to be about as ancient as possible for that kind of technology. The images were dark and grainy but two of the outside cameras would light up with a blue edging around the image if the motion sensor picked up something and it started recording. One of the things I'd been warned about in training was that it was common thing for that camera to turn on and for nothing to be there.

I tried to take that warning to heart and remind myself that it was probably just a squirrel or possum or other small animal that was trig-gering the motion sensor but was too small for the camera to actually capture. In general, I did my best to ignore the cameras because they made me feel more on edge than anything else in the store. I told myself it was just because I was alone in the middle of nowhere.

I'd been at that job for two months when I saw a car pull up in front of the store. I put away the college acceptance letter I'd gotten and planned to decline. The deadline was coming up and I'd decided to take a year off.

I saw someone get out of the car and start to head for the door. They'd parked out of sight of the cameras.

I only looked up when the buzzer sounded and I automatically hit the button to unlock the door for the person to come in. I ducked down behind the desk quickly to put my letter away.

"Hey, Mia."

I stood up so quickly I almost fell backwards. "Dan?" I stared at him. My first instinct was to jump the counter and tackle him. I couldn't decide whether to punch him or hug him. "Where the hell have you been?"

He smiled slightly but there was an edge of something to it that I couldn't place. "What are you doing here?"

I stared at him some more. "Working. Obviously. Where have you been? It's been *months!*" I was suddenly furious. How dare he just walk in here like nothing after we'd spent so much time looking for him.

The smile faded from his face. "Was that your college acceptance letter? You're going, aren't you?"

"No," I said right away. Then I shook my head. "I- I don't know. I wasn't going to because I wanted to help your mom look for you. She's out of her mind, you know."

His expression shifted and somehow he looked both sad and touched at the same time. "You need to go to school. My mom'll be fine. Everyone'll be fine. Promise me you'll go to school."

"Why should I promise you anything?" I was still angry. This idiot had been my best friend growing up and now he didn't even have the decency to tell me what he'd been doing for months.

"Mia. Promise me you'll go to school. This year. No matter what happens."

I suddenly felt cold. I found myself nodding before I could even really think about it. "I... Yeah. Ok, I'll go to school."

He smiled but there was that edge of something else behind it again. "You're going to kick ass. Everyone's going to be so proud of you when you graduate. Don't let anything stop you. Promise me."

"Dan, what's going on?"

He glanced toward the car. I couldn't see it very well but it was a red sedan. It looked like the license plate was blue but I couldn't see any of the numbers.

"Just promise me."

I nodded again. "I promise. I'll kick ass and you better be at my graduation cheering for me."

"I love you, Mia."

I frowned and he started to go. "Where are you going?"

He waved at me and he was out the door before I even realized what was going on. I sprinted after him in time to see him get into the passenger seat of the little red car. They drove off before I could try and say anything else.

I stood in the doorway for a long time until someone else came to the store and I had to help them. I could have called my aunt to tell her what happened but decided it was a conversation to have in person.

I finished off my shift and went straight to her house when I was done. I was ready to tell her what happened. Then I noticed the police car sitting out front.

My stomach twisted nervously and I went inside. Everything that came next was a bit of a blur.

I sat on the couch with my aunt. She was crying. One of the officers was talking to her but I couldn't quite understand what about.

Then I realized it was because he was talking about my cousin in past tense. I wanted to tell them that was silly, that they didn't know what they were doing. I'd just spoken to Dan.

The other officer started talking. I think he was trying to tell me something but I felt too detached. Suddenly it hit me.

The officers were telling me and my aunt they'd found my cousin. They'd found Dan's body, badly decomposed, a few towns over near a red sedan.

I tried to tell them I'd just spoken to him. Or at least I thought I did. They didn't seem to understand me. Or maybe I was the one not understanding them.

The next thing I knew the officers were gone. Some of my other family showed up and I was able to excuse myself to a quiet room.

None of it made sense. I couldn't be sure it ever would. I finally decided not to tell anyone about what had happened, the same way I didn't tell them about the way time flowed differently in parts of the store, or the footprints I couldn't explain.

I took the acceptance letter out of my bag and filled it out, agreeing to attend in the fall. While the rest of my family was in the other room mourning my cousin I took the letter out to the mailbox to fulfill my promise to Dan.

FROM THE INSIDE

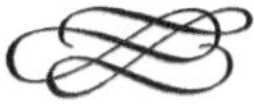

The alarms blaring in the cockpit were the only thing keeping Sarai grounded. Or rather, keeping her focused on what she had to do. The temperature in the starfighter rose quickly.

She tried to reach for the shield controls to reroute whatever power she could to them. The inertia of the fighter's end over end tumble made it nearly impossible for her to stretch even the few inches.

As the starfighter continued to roll through the atmosphere a sudden gust stopped the uncontrolled spin just for a moment.

Sarai's fist slammed into the controls. The protective shields surrounded the ship. Then the last bit of energy going to the engines failed and she lost all control as the ship fell to the surface of the planet below.

Despite the protective suit Sarai's vision blacked out completely.

* * *

SARAI DIDN'T EXPECT to open her eyes again. When she did it took her a moment to focus. Everything was blurry and tinged with red.

Blood?

No, not blood. Dirt. It smeared the visor of her helmet. Somehow she was thrown from the cockpit of the fighter. As she pushed herself up slowly she realized she hadn't just been flung from the cockpit. The ejection pod had deployed sometime after she'd lost consciousness. Her stomach sank.

Her vision swam out of focus as she pushed to her feet. She willed herself to stay steady so she could look around. Not too far away she spotted the ejection pod. There was a large drag mark in the red dirt where she'd apparently pulled herself away. She took in the rest of the surroundings.

Wind whipped more of the red dirt through the air. There were a few bent and broken pieces of alloy spread in the area.

Sarai didn't have to look much more to know what happened. She wouldn't be using that ship to leave the planet. That was fine, she had a communicator. The rest of the fleet was still in orbit. When she'd been hit the battle had just turned in their favor. All she had to do was signal and they'd send a pickup transport as soon as it was clear.

She checked the systems control panel on her forearm. Her oxygen level was solid. It also told her that the planet was cold. The suit's heater would kick in soon. That would take a lot of energy. She did a few mental calculations. All told she had enough for eight hours. More than enough time for a rescue transport.

She activated the communicator. The HUD on her visor blinked red and she frowned at it. There was no signal.

"Of course not," she muttered. That was going to make rescue difficult.

A quick scan of the area showed her there was a nearby mountain range. It wasn't that steep and seemed completely climbable. With a heavy sigh Sarai turned that way.

* * *

SARAI HAD BARELY STARTED up the mountain when she realized she was in trouble. There were tracks in the dirt. They had already been half blown away by the wind but this planet hadn't been listed as having any sentient life. And she knew those tracks.

"Ok, you bastard, we'll see who gets there first."

* * *

Hearing in the life support suit wasn't great in the best conditions. Add in the wind and Sarai could barely hear her own footsteps.

Somehow she managed to hear the skitter of dirt and rocks off to the side. She turned and tried to locate the source.

The flash of the carapace was all the warning she had. She ducked instinctively and hit the ground. As she rolled onto her back she saw the shadow soar over her. The sound of spindly legs hitting the dirt was off to the side and she scrambled for something to use to fend off the alien. Her hand closed around a large rock and she threw it before she'd even fully lined up a clear shot.

There was a dull *thunk* and Sarai squinted to see past the dust in the air. All she saw were a few legs as the alien skittered away behind a large outcropping of rocks.

Sarai didn't wait. She bolted in the opposite direction. She slid on the smaller rocks and dust of the planet as well as struggled against the strong wind.

Few people had ever engaged one of the Cascara in a hand-to-hand fight or even a fight on the ground. Their strength clearly lay in space where they superior ships generally made short work of even the best technology Earth had to offer.

As Sarai sprinted away a thought occurred to her. She hadn't damaged the other ship. Not enough for it to have crashed on the planet with her.

* * *

Luckily for Sarai the Cascara weren't known for hand to hand combat. The war against them had been almost exclusively been in air combat and the rock had clearly chased it off enough that it didn't come after her again.

Tracking the ship down had been another stroke of luck. She'd been able to follow the tracks almost directly to it before they got blown away.

Sarai just made her way up to it when something hit her from behind. She fell forward and felt something in her chest pop as she hit a rock. Or maybe it was something in her suit. Adrenaline surged and she flailed, trying to shake the weight off her. She rolled onto her back and kicked out wildly.

Everything happened quickly and Sarai wasn't entirely sure how it happened but after a brief struggle the Cascara skittered away and Sarai was just aware of some kind of sickly clicking sound that the alien was making.

She went after it with the heavy rock. A few moments later the Cascara was on the ground unmoving. Its multiple spindly legs were curled in on itself and it looked unnervingly like a giant dead bug.

As she straightened she caught sight of the systems control panel on her suit. Something had gotten damaged in the struggle.

She only had a few hours of oxygen left.

Cursing loudly, Sarai scanned the area and did another check of her communication system.

She ran for the ship instead. No one had ever flown a Cascara ship before but she wasn't going to let that stop her. If anyone could fly it, it was her.

She forced herself to keep her breathing calm, doing every trick she knew even as she scurried around the ship and searched for a way in.

The ship looked more like some kind of pod. It reminded her of the pods that baby sharks were born out of. As she crawled underneath it to look for a way in a slit appeared in the belly of the ship.

Sarai slithered her way inside and tried to check for the oxygen content in the ship. It was no better than outside which meant she was going to have to hurry.

The next hour was a struggle. Sarai tried to make sense of the inside of the pod while kept her breathing even. She couldn't afford to waste what oxygen she had left. She periodically checked her communicator but there was still no sign of any rescue.

"Fine. I can get myself off this rock."

An alarm on the suit system flashed. Her oxygen levels were critical.

She gritted her teeth and set back to work. The pod controls were clearly designed to be used by multiple limbs at once. She poked at them and prodded in frustration. Her chest felt tight.

After some more maneuvering the ship suddenly shuddered and her stomach lurched as it moved. Beneath her the slit closed and she resisted a shout of triumph.

The controls needed to be worked with her hands and feet and some extra stretching but since Sarai was laying on her stomach she could just about make it. The inside of the pod became slightly transparent and her stomach swooped again as she saw it lift off the surface of the planet.

It was the most disconcerting thing Sarai had ever experienced. Even with all her fighter training and simulations it was hard to fight the gut reaction that the ship around her was disappearing and she needed to do *something*.

Maneuvering the ship took just as much effort. She let it hover as she worked out the directional controls. The sparkles floating in her vision signaled she didn't have a lot of time.

The ship rattled hard as it charged through the atmosphere and she had to struggle to stay in place and reach the controls necessary to work the fighter.

There were no mechanical scanners, not that Sarai had been able to work out, but that wasn't an issue since she could see nearly the entirety of space around her.

She picked up her visual scanning and searched for her fleet. They had to be in the area; they would be scanning the planet and looking for her and her ship.

As the seconds passed and she didn't see anything her heart started to pound in her chest. They had to be here. There was no sign of debris and she knew that if there had been a battle she would still see it. There would be ships and scattered pieces or even bodies. And there was nothing.

Panic settled in her chest. There wasn't a lot of time left in her suit. She searched the ship for something, anything, she could use. After a moment she just sagged forward and let her helmet fall into her hands. Her shoulders trembled and black started to edge into her vision.

She started to calm herself. *So this is it,* she thought when the ship shuddered. It wasn't much at first and she assumed it was just shifting because she'd let go of the controls.

Then the ship shuddered so hard she nearly rolled off the perch she'd been laying on that passed for a seat in the ship. Sarai twisted to look behind her. Through the transparent portions of the ship she saw the form of another larger ship. It nearly blocked out all of the stars and the planet behind her.

As she reached to settle back and take the controls again she realized the ship was moving backwards towards the giant ship. She cursed and tried to regain control. She looked back again to gauge how much time she had.

Then she recognized something. There was a patch of light that was growing and she scrambled to sit up.

As she did the pod slowly entered the hangar of the larger ship. Her breathing was labored but she knew she just had to hold on a little while longer.

The pod settled on the deck. Sarai flopped around as she struggled to figure out how to reopen the pod. When the slit opened she went tumbling onto the deck.

Figures moved towards her as Sarai tried to regain her bearings. She reached up to unfasten her helmet but her fingers wouldn't quite cooperate.

She found herself surrounded as one of the figures pulled the helmet off.

Cool, stale air swept over Sarai's face and she gasped. She squinted and scanned the people that had surrounded her. There were members of the deck crew as well as a few other pilots.

The face of her second in command swam into view and she smiled down at Sarai.

"Welcome home."

PLAY WITH ME, PART 1

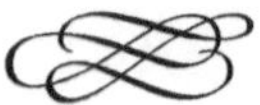

"We have everything, right?"

I sighed and nodded. "Yeah, I checked the pack twice. And I made copies of the instructions and we should have plenty of batteries and matches."

"Should?" Mariana looked at me severely.

"Definitely have enough." My voice was firm and somehow it didn't betray that I was shaking already.

I kept up right behind Mariana. My little sister was braver than I was and most days it grated on me. For now, I was just glad to have her with me.

Our town had always had stories of weird things going on. Missing people that the police could never pick up solid leads for. Local legends about creatures that roamed the dense woods that practically surrounded the town. The latest pairs of missing hikers had finally pushed us into acting.

We had a list of things we thought it could be but the only way to narrow it down and know for sure was to get out there ourselves.

When we got to the location where the hikers had set up their camp Mariana and I stopped to pull things out of our bags. While she used a flashlight to check the campsite, which was still wrapped in police tape, I yanked my phone out and decided to take advantage of the signal to get better access to a list of monsters.

"Okay, well, it's not likely to be a wendigo. Those would probably be leaving body parts everywhere," I said as I scrolled the list. "Rougarou?"

"I thought those were Louisiana based," my sister said as she searched.

I made a face at her. "Mothman?"

"That was never associated with any disappearances."

"We're running low on woods-based monsters here," I told her.

"Maybe it's a lake monster."

"I dunno, this camp site is pretty far from the lake."

"They could have hiked it, though. Maybe they stayed out too late and got caught in the dark on the way back."

I nodded slowly. "That would mean they didn't go missing here at camp, it would have been somewhere along the trail to the lake."

My sister finished poking around in the tents and looked over at me. Even though she was shining the flashlight towards me and I was half blinded from looking at my phone I could tell she was grinning. "Then we should take a walk to the lake."

I nodded my agreement, despite my hesitation, and we started off down the trail.

"If it is a lake monster don't you think the police would have found something the last time they dragged the lake?" I skipped forward a few steps to get even with Mariana.

"Look, Rocio, I get that you don't believe in this stuff. So why are you here with me?"

"I never said I don't believe in this stuff," I said. "I just don't fully buy it is all. But I'm here and I'm just trying to understand so we know what we're getting into here."

I could see her thinking that over. Somewhere in the distance I heard a noise. Mariana must have heard it too because she looked up and seemed to concentrate.

"Sounds like crying," she said.

"One of the hikers?"

Mariana shook her head and turned off the trail to go towards the sound.

"Ok, that's a terrible idea, that's like the first step to getting murdered," I said but followed after her.

The crying seemed to get louder and it was definitely not an adult.

"Sounds like a kid. What would a kid be doing out here in the middle of the night?"

"You're technically a kid and here you are," I informed her. I doubted any monsters in the woods would care that I'd just turned eighteen if they were the type to like tasty little kids.

"I'm a teenager," she informed me loftily.

We both slowed to a stop as the crying faded. Marina shone the flashlight around in an attempt to see anything.

"It's just us," I said but kept my voice quiet. I suddenly was very afraid of attracting attention to ourselves.

For another long moment we were quiet and strained to hear anything. There was some wind that gently rustled the trees but that was it.

"Did you hear that?" Mariana asked, voice barely above a whisper.

"What? No."

"Someone said my name."

I bit my lip. "Maybe we should go back."

She shook her head and before I knew it she'd taken off through the trees.

"Mari! Mariana!" I hurried after her. "Mariana Guadalupe, get back here!"

She ignored me and somehow seemed to be putting distance on me. A moment later her flashlight beam disappeared from sight.

I froze in place, old memories of our mom telling me that if I ever got lost to stay where I was surfaced in my memory. Except I was the adult here, I had to look for my sister.

"Mariana!" I took off again after her, using my cell phone flashlight to see where I was going. Behind me I heard someone giggle and the hair on the back of my neck stood on end. "Mariana?" I turned and shone the light to try and see.

I heard the giggle again.

I spun and tried to locate the sound but it was either echoing or the sound was moving.

"Let's play a game," a voice said. A voice that sounded like it was right next to my ear.

I yelped and spun but no one was there.

"You hide. I seek."

My heart pounded so loud I almost couldn't hear the voice. But it definitely sounded like a little boy. Something about it was familiar but I was too terrified to think it through. Instead I picked a direction and ran like my life depended on it. Which, at that moment, felt like it did.

I didn't think about where I was going and for the moment Mariana was forgotten in my panic. I burst out of the trees into a small clearing. My foot caught on something and I went down hard. My phone slid away. The light was shining into the dirt and it was suddenly dark all around me except for the small sliver of moonlight from the sky.

As I rolled onto my back I saw something off to the side. I looked and could just make out a shadow. It was short, like a little kid.

"Found you."

I pushed away, or at least tried to, and felt small twigs and dried leaves poking at me from the ground. I stared at the form in some hope it would just vanish. "Go away!"

"Why won't you play with me?" The form shifted and melted away.

For a moment I thought I was clear but when I turned the shadow had moved to my other side and was much closer.

"Play." The voice was more familiar now.

"Hector?" I didn't want to believe it and even through my fear I felt stupid for saying it.

"Rocio."

I felt like the temperature had dropped a full thirty degrees. Blindly I scrambled to my feet and turned to run back into the trees. Before I'd even gone one step the shadow was in front of me. It was no taller than a four-year-old, the same age Hector had been.

"Go away!" I shouted again. "Just leave us alone! You're dead!"

The shadow flickered again and for a moment I thought maybe that had worked.

"Mari will play with me."

I opened my mouth to protest, to tell Hector…no, the spirit…to leave our sister alone. The shadow surged forward and I felt like I'd been submerged into a pool of ice water. Everything went dark.

* * *

MY EYELIDS WERE SO heavy I couldn't lift them but I could hear a conversation going on even though it sounded distant, like I was hearing it from the far end of a tunnel.

"... suffering from exposure, do you have any idea what she was doing?"

"No… her sister? Where is…"

"Disappeared… no sign of her…"

I wanted to wake up more then and ask what was going on. But a part of me already knew.

As I felt unconsciousness tug at me again Hector's voice echoed in my mind.

Mari will play with me.

And I knew I'd never see my sister or little brother again.

SHOOTING GHOSTS

"Ok, do the intro again."

Dom sighed heavily and turned back to face me. "The first intro was fine. Let's just get some footage of getting inside. We have to do the history of it and all."

I sighed right back but didn't push the issue. Our channel was just starting to get popular and I knew it was mostly due to his choices and the fact that he was the face of it. I only pushed the issue when it came to making sure we got certain shots and had plenty of footage to splice together. Editing was my main job.

"Ok, we do need a shot of you going in."

"I know, but I need to mess with the lock first."

"I thought you said you snagged the key from your mom."

"I did, but I don't want that on camera."

I shrugged. I could edit it but I understood his paranoia.

I waited for Dom to deal with the lock. I took some outdoor footage while I waited.

I had a flashlight attachment for the camera so I alternated using it and taking advantage of the night vision setting.

Dom did his standard intro as we went in. He talked about how exciting the video was going to be. As we stood in the doorway he turned back and I automatically lifted the camera.

"Per our usual ghost hunting expedition we have Kat with the camera, we each have flashlights with fresh batteries and our cell phones are fully charged for our evening in the house. We also brought some snacks in case we need to use them as an offering."

We toured the house first. Three bedrooms, two bathrooms. Naturally a basement and an attic. One of the bedrooms was locked, though, or at least jammed closed so tightly we couldn't get in.

Dom made a few attempts to speak out to the ghosts as we went. As I took a break from filming I looked in one of the boxes in the bedroom.

"Hey, Dom," I started, pulling a diary out. When I turned he was gone so I shoved the diary into my pocket as I went to go find him.

* * *

FOR THE NEXT hour we wandered the house. I filmed Dom as he called out to the ghosts and spirits and I stood by a few walls to kick at them. I tried to wait and catch Dom as much off guard as I could to try and get the most startled reaction I could.

When I said we'd filmed enough we went to the living room to eat some of the snacks we'd brought for the night. We talked a little and then Dom went to go see what kind of props we could rig up to fall at just the right times and such for more footage.

Technically we didn't have to spend all night but it wasn't like anyone would notice we were missing for the night.

Once he was gone I pulled out the diary and opened it to begin to read. I skimmed it, feeling suddenly guilty for reading it.

Next month is my birthday. I asked if I could spend some time with some friends to celebrate. Mother said no, as if she knows there isn't anyone I could spend time with.

Oh good. I had managed to find the super angsty diary of some teenager. I went to turn the page and something heavy hit the ground upstairs and I jumped so high I stumbled off the chair I'd been sitting in.

"Dom?" I went to go find him.

He was face first on the ground, half of him sticking out from one of the doorways.

"Fine, I'm fine," he groaned and pushed himself up.

"Wasn't that door locked earlier?"

"Thought so. I leaned against it to see if I could get any good footage from my phone and it just opened and I went down."

I brought the camera up to film as I stepped inside. Immediately I could see this room was different. It was still mostly furnished, like the rest of the house, but there were drawings and completely illegible scribblings all over the walls.

"That's definitely not creepy at all," Dom muttered. He brushed his fingers against the scribbling. "Is anyone here? Any ghosts or spirits with us, give us a sign."

A door squeaked open back out in the hallway and we both spun towards the sound.

I hurried out, still filming, to take a look. We both checked out the area but didn't see anything.

Eventually we went back downstairs.

* * *

DOM FLOPPED down on the living room couch and messed around on his phone for a while.

I pulled out the diary again and flipped to the next entry.

I can hear them fighting downstairs. Mother's crying. She's insisting something's wrong with the house. He's mad because he says it's bad enough that I complained about moving in the middle of the school year. She says she hears things at night and that he would know if he was ever around. I've shut myself in my closet but I can still hear her crying.

There was a yell and when I jumped the diary slid off my lap.

Across the room from me Dom had yelped and fallen off the couch.

"What? What is it?" I tried to look around in the dark to see what had startled him.

He scrambled back away from the couch and was breathing hard. "I thought...I saw...I mean, I was on my phone and...and I was messing with the camera and it said it recognized a face in the dark," he sputtered.

My heart pounded in my chest. Neither of us believed in ghosts, not really, but we still liked a good ghost story. For a second I thought he was just trying to put on a good show for me. I grabbed the camera and started filming.

"Dom, why don't you explain what just happened and we'll go take a look."

His eyes were still wide and everything looked green and dark in the camera's night vision setting. He explained again what had happened and then we took a quick peek around the lower floor of the house. For effect I made some subtle banging noises while we were in the kitchen.

"I'm going to head into the attic. I'll set up some stuff to fall over and then maybe we call it a night."

"Chicken," I teased but didn't argue. I let him go off and I sat in the kitchen to pull out the diary. It was back in my pocket although I didn't remember putting it there.

When I got home Mother was gone. Father said he took her to get some help. That the stress of the move made her sick. I wanted to tell him that I felt something shake my bed last night but I don't want him to send me away too.

The hair on the back of my neck stood on end and I straightened. The diary hit the ground with a dull thud. I reached for my phone this time.

"Hello?" I hoped it wasn't Dom trying to scare me or I was going to kick his ass. I turned the camera feature on as I walked, the lit flashlight in my other hand.

I made my way up to the attic to find Dom. As I approached the pull-down ladder my phone camera slid past one of the open bedroom doors. The square that indicated the phone was trying to focus on a face appeared and I jumped. I turned that way as my flash-light flickered.

I thought I made out a shadow and two glowing orbs by the far window.

I blinked and it was gone.

* * *

DOM WASN'T able to figure out how to rig anything in the attic to move so he went to try the basement instead. He figured the rafters would give us a good opportunity.

Curiosity made me pull the diary from my pocket. I sat on the basement stairs as he worked.

I saw the creature Mother mentioned the other day. I woke up because of the cold in my room. When I opened my eyes I saw something staring at me in the dark. It was just a shadow but its eyes glowed. I wanted to yell but I couldn't move. When I blinked it was gone and the temperature went back to normal.

I felt like I'd gone cold as well. "Dom?" I said, my voice sounding small.

"Hang on, Kat."

"No, it's important," I insisted more urgently. Upstairs there was a loud thud, or maybe more than one, and we both jumped.

I raced up the stairs ahead of Dom. At first the living room looked like nothing had been touched but the furniture was just slightly out of place and one of the dining room chairs had fallen over.

"Ok, just a chair," he said but his voice was trembling. "Nothing to worry about."

"Dom, all the furniture moved."

"Get the camera out."

My hands were shaking but I brought the camera up. I had it hanging around my neck from the cord and I was suddenly very aware of the diary in my back pocket. I hadn't put it there when we came upstairs, had I?

"So, Kat and I were just downstairs in the basement when we

heard something crash. We came up and all the furniture's moved just a little and this chair fell over."

I panned the camera around the house.

"Thing is, the noise was louder. Like all the furniture got dropped at once. This is getting serious, guys."

As the camera's view settled near the stairs up I screamed.

The shadow with the two glowing eyes was there.

Dom scrambled over as I skittered back away, nearly dropping the camera if it hadn't been hanging around my neck. "What? What is it?"

"I saw it again!"

"Saw what?"

I didn't answer. Instead I headed for the stairs and tried to ignore the way my heart pounded in my chest. I held the camera up as I searched for any other sign of the shadow.

I couldn't find it and I could see Dom was starting to think I was pranking him or maybe just going crazy.

* * *

I TOLD Dom I needed a break and was going to get some air outside. I stood by the front door and read the diary using my flashlight.

Mother came home. She's been back for days. Father's stayed home to care for her and help her readjust to being back. I tried to get in to see her but he won't let me. I caught a small glimpse of her room. There are scribblings and odd drawings all over the walls now.

The room upstairs immediately popped to my mind. I shut the diary and put it back in my pocket and went to find Dom. I had to tell him what I found.

I left the kitchen and when I got to the stairs I looked up and tried to figure out where Dom could be. As I looked up I saw someone standing there. I shone my flashlight that way.

For an instant I saw a girl, her hair hung in greasy strands and she wore only a long gray t-shirt that was a number of sizes too big for her. I started and the flashlight briefly moved off her. When I moved the light back she was gone.

"Dom?"

"Up here," he called.

I started up the stairs. I'd barely made it halfway when I heard a shout. It cut off abruptly as it turned into a kind of strangled gurgling sound followed by a thump and then nothing.

I froze for a second but then rushed up the stairs. "Dom? Dom!" I searched the rooms and didn't find anything.

I headed to the room where all the writing was and felt as though the temperature dropped about ten degrees.

The walls were now not only covered in drawings and scribbles but spattered blood.

I backed up quickly. "Dom?" I could hear my voice shaking. It was only appropriate since the rest of me was shaking as well. I turned to go back downstairs. I had to get out of the house. I had to get help.

I threw myself at the front door. When it didn't budge I pounded on it hard and shouted.

Even as I did I knew no one would hear me. We'd picked the house because it was the only one on a dead-end street so no one would notice us hanging around while we filmed.

I grabbed the camera and turned it on to keep filming.

"Ok, I'm apparently locked in. Dom's missing and I...I found a lot of blood." If I narrated what was going on I could manage the shaking. And the fear. It felt like one of our usual shoots where half of what we did was faked and the other half was just us jumping at our shadows.

I turned slowly and filmed the inside of the house again. I was going to go upstairs when I caught sight of the shadow again. I could see it more clearly this time. It was clearly a tall human shape and the eyes glowed brighter than I'd seen so far.

And it didn't disappear when I blinked.

Without thinking I sprinted down the basement steps. I tripped down the last few and the camera tumbled from my hands. I didn't go after it. Instead I crawled to one corner of the basement. As I stared towards the stairs the shadow reappeared out of nowhere.

The temperature plummeted again and I froze in place. The shadow started towards me.

Behind it I suddenly made out another figure. It was the girl from earlier.

There was some kind of screech that hurt my ears so badly I clapped my hands over my ears. The girl rushed forward but her legs never moved and her image flickered slightly and like she would stop existing for brief periods of time only to reappear a split second later.

Then she collided with the shadow and there was a flash of light so bright my eyes hurt.

I curled up on the floor in an attempt to cover my ears and keep my eyes closed.

The room was suddenly quiet and the temperature seemed to slowly go back up.

When I opened my eyes there was only the dark of the basement. I tried my flashlight and it flickered back to life but was dim. So much for fresh batteries.

I sat back and felt the diary in my pocket. Automatically I pulled it out again and read the last entry.

He's finally done it. I heard crying and I left my room to see what was going on. The bedroom door was open just enough that I could see inside. He had a knife and Mother was on the ground. There was blood. So much blood. I've hidden in my room but I can hear him. He's coming for me.

I put the diary aside. I didn't know what to think. I was shaking too hard to even think about moving.

It wasn't until sometime later, when the first bits of light started to come through the basement windows, that I dared move. I grabbed the camera and made my way back upstairs. I had no idea what to do first or if anyone would even believe me or what had happened to Dom.

The only thing I knew was that this would be the last video I ever filmed.

PROTECTING THE WRECK

"Zara, you know there's a reason this station was abandoned," her unofficial second-in-command said.

"I've heard the old ghost stories," she said. She led the way further into the station. The power was out so they had to wear their protective suits. As they passed one of the windows it was an admittedly impressive sight. There were stars as far as the eye could see and since the station hung in a remote location there was no other traffic or even any obvious planets nearby. "Don't tell me you believe them."

"I don't *not* believe them," he said simply. "You live in space. How do you not believe in ghosts?"

"Rowan. I live in space because science is provable and repeatable. Ghosts are not." The captain, unofficial though her title was, smiled sweetly at him and went to finish checking the station for any mechanic problems that needed to get fixed.

A few hours later the power was on and the rest of the crew was unloading things in their new home.

* * *

ZARA LOVED LIVING IN SPACE. She knew that it was a privilege not everyone got to experience. Sure, most short distance space vehicles were almost commonplace these days but the cost of maintaining a private spaceship of the size she needed was expensive. Normally it housed her, Rowan, and twin siblings Kiara and Amari. But fewer jobs were becoming available to them so Zara needed a place for them to live that was a little more self-sustainable than a modified cargo transport.

Which was why she chose an abandoned space station. There were a few systems that needed repair, but the life support functioned and it had enough space to stretch out a little. Everyone got more living space as well as designated areas to grow and store food.

Zara loved it.

What she didn't love was how quickly Rowan's ridiculous superstitions spread through the rest of the crew.

Flickering lights became evidence of a ghost rather than faulty power levels across the station.

Thumps or bumps that were normal sounds in a station of that size became angry signs.

The worst part was everyone buying into it. Except Zara. She refused.

For the most part the others kept up with their duties. Rowan refused to go near Deck 4 without an escort and complained that something had to have happened in the hallway by the main airlock because it was always so cold.

Zara had tried telling him that of *course* it was cold there. The insulation needed to be re-installed properly and space is cold.

She told herself that once the repairs were done things would settle down and everyone would stop insisting their new home was haunted.

* * *

A SCREAM WOKE Zara in the middle of the night. She tried to get out of her bunk so quickly that she got herself tangled in her sheets and slammed her knee hard into the ground. As pain shot up her leg she pushed back to her feet and limped into the hallway.

Amari, already in the corridor, looked around for the source of the scream. "Was that Kiara?"

"I don't know," Zara said, trying not to sound impatient. They sprinted towards the sound.

They found Kiara sprawled on the floor by the airlock staring at nothing in particular.

"What happened? Are you alright?" Amari knelt at her sister's side.

"I saw it!" Kiara stammered and pointed at the dark but empty hall in front of her.

Zara groaned.

"Saw what?" Amari asked.

"Nothing," Zara immediately put in. "She saw nothing because *nothing* was there!"

"No, there was definitely something! It was a guy, or at least, y'know, a guy-looking form and half his face was missing!" Kiara tripped over her words in her panic but still remembered to catch herself with her pronoun usage. Having Amari for her twin meant that was a consideration she kept in mind even in moments of stress.

"There was no one," Zara insisted, but Kiara looked up at her with wide eyes. She ground her teeth together. "Amari, take your sister and make a sweep around that way. I'll head the other way and meet you on the other side at the control panel."

"I knew I should have gotten those internal scanners up and running," ze said.

"You can work on it tomorrow. Now let's go."

Kiara got to her feet with Amari's help. "You shouldn't go alone."

Zara ignored her and started down the hall.

A few minutes later they'd made the loop around the station and met each other at one of the control panels.

"Well, just like I thought. Nothing." Zara couldn't help the slight bitterness coloring her tone. Her knee ached fiercely and their insistence on ghosts haunting the station was tiring. If they were worried enough about the imagined ghosts that they were now hallucinating she had to do something about it.

Kiara's eyes were wide and worried. "Zara, I swear, I wasn't hallucinating or imagining it. He…they…*someone* was there."

Zara sighed and looked at the system panel they'd met at. "Go back to bed, both of you. I'll do a system scan and check for any anomalies or power surges."

"Zara…"

"I mean it. I'll let you know in the morning what I find."

Kiara looked guilty but Amari put an arm around her shoulders and steered them back down the hallway.

With a sigh Zara set to work going through the system logs to look for anything she could use to settle her crew's fears.

* * *

As Zara went into the ship's logs she dug deeper to find old recordings and records that she hadn't bothered looking at when they first arrived. Now, though, she knew she had to find something to ease their minds.

The first log she came across was the newest and seemed to have been recorded around the time the station was abandoned.

Zara started with the text. All it said was that a ship had been spotted in the area but had ignored all attempts at contact. It didn't appeared to be armed, but maintained a course towards the station.

Then Zara opened a video file.

An image of a woman a few years older than Zara appeared. A cut across her forehead bled profusely and her eyes were wide with terror.

"I'm leaving this log in the ship's computer for anyone who comes later. My name is Astrid and I'm in charge of this station. My crew, fourteen others, are all-" Her voice cracked and she looked down for a moment. Then she steeled herself and looked up once again.

"My crew is dead. I've included the schematics of the ship that attacked us. They didn't have any weapons and we believed they needed aid. When we

let them on board they attacked. We tried to hide and hold them off but we weren't equipped. We never wanted to fight. We only wanted to live away from others and away from trouble."

Zara felt a lump form in her throat.

"I'm the only one left and I know they're going to come find me. My only hope is that they will face justice. In this life or the next."

Something loud banged in the background and the woman turned. Someone was standing behind her. He lifted something that looked like a thick bat and then the recording cut out.

* * *

ZARA DECIDED to keep the find to herself. She made copies of all the files and then wiped everything from the station's systems.

Amari and Kiara pressed her for any information, but Zara brushed them off and made it clear the subject was not going to be brought up again.

The last thing she needed was for them to tell Rowan and for the three of them to insist that the ghosts haunting the place were really the spirits of the ones who'd been killed at the station.

She kept all the information on the attack, though. If a group like that had come through before then she wanted to know about it in case they decided to swing by again.

* * *

THEY LIVED at the station for a few months when the station sent a proximity alarm alert to Zara's room . She'd set it to notify her first but she'd never expected it to ever actually go off.

When she woke herself enough to check on the report her heart skipped a beat. There wasn't nearly enough time for them to prepare.

Zara ran down the hallway and banged hard on the cabin doors. "Up! Everyone up! This is no drill!"

Slowly the cabin doors slid open and the sleepy faces of her crew emerged to greet her.

Zara didn't let them ask questions.

"Rowan. Get to the ship, get her going. Kiara, you grab what food supplies you can and as much of it as you can get to the ship in ten minutes. Amari, I need you with me and collecting anything we can use as a weapon. Help me seal the station."

They all started talking at once and Zara could have strangled them.

"That's an order!"

Rowan raised a hand. "Cap, look, I can't get the ship going, I wasn't able to finish those repairs. The engine'll run but we won't get anywhere."

Zara cursed. "How long to finish the repairs?"

"A few hours?"

"Why the hell did you leave the ship in pieces?"

Rowan shrugged helplessly. "What's going on?"

"I don't have time to explain. Fine, new orders. Everyone grab what weapons you can and then hide. You don't come out for anything. Anything. You understand?"

This time they didn't argue. There was a flurry of activity as they all skittered off to do as they were told.

The one problem with the station was that they didn't really have any weapons. Zara grabbed a heavy tool that she could swing with one hand and then headed for the airlock to greet their visitors.

On the way there the lights flickered. Zara could have sworn that Rowan had said he'd stabilized the power fluctuations in that hallway. The temperature dropped noticeably and Zara privately thought it was probably better they hadn't managed to put too much money into fixing that particular issue. None of them might be around much longer to enjoy it.

She stood in the middle of the hallway in front of the airlock. She could hear the gears and life support system working to accommodate the ship on the other side.

The door slid open and a group of half a dozen men stood there. Their spacesuits were decorated in symbols that Zara didn't recognize and had various strips of cloth hanging from them. When she looked closer she saw some braids and what appeared to be bits of bone hanging as necklaces or just dangling from the arms or legs from some of the men's suits.

The man in front didn't even seem surprised to see Zara. He looked her up and down as though she was a meal to be assessed rather than a person. Her grip on the heavy tool stayed strong.

"I'll give you one warning. Turn back now," she said flatly. This was her home. The people inside were her family. And she had always known that if it came down to it she would die to protect them.

The men exchanged glances and then started laughing.

"Not a chance," the front man said simply. As he went to take a step forward the entire area suddenly plunged into darkness.

Even Zara jumped and she blinked furiously to try and get her eyes to adjust. The only light was now coming in through a few small windows filled with the stars.

She stepped back against the far part of the hall. She could hear more than see the men shuffling around. The bits of bones they wore made a distinctive sound as they moved.

"If you think a little darkness is going to scare us..." He stepped forward and suddenly there was a high-pitched scream.

Zara's hair stood on end as she turned towards the sound. A few yards down the hall stood a woman.

She had a cut across her forehead that spilled blood down the side of her face. She was unarmed but her face was a mask of fury. She flickered in and out of existence.

The temperature dropped even further. Zara was just aware of her breath.

One of the men threw something toward the woman. She flickered and disappeared.

They seemed stunned and muttered to each other but Zara could hear the panic in their voices. She readied herself and was about to charge the leader when she spotted movement out of the corner of her eye. Her instincts told her it was the rest of her crew and her stomach sank.

When she turned to look, though, she didn't recognize any of the people standing there. One was bleeding heavily from a wound that seemed to have taken off most of his face.

There was a large group of them, too many for Zara to count. They charged forward, hovering across the distance and it felt as though a bitter winter wind rushed through the hallway.

Zara dropped to her knees and covered her head with her arms. She didn't dare move.

Then she became aware of the sound of the airlock cycling. When she looked up she saw the other ship floating away. There was something wrong with it. When something thudded against the small window Zara barely held back a yelp of surprise.

It was one of the men that had just been threatening her and the station. As she approached the tiny window she could see all the others drifting in space.

The lights came on as suddenly as they'd gone out and the temperature rose to normal.

Zara stood there for a long moment. She looked up and down the hallway but the light held strong and the warmth of the area was unusual. She turned slowly and saw the woman from the recording. She stood at the far end of the corridor.

"Thank you," Zara said.

The woman smiled, flickered, and then disappeared.

She took a deep breath and then waited a few minutes for the bodies and the ship outside to drift away. Once she was satisfied, she turned to find her crew and let them know that they were safe.

MOVING DAY

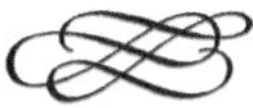

The first time we moved I was seven. I'd been in school for a month and it was the most exciting time. I hadn't gone to school before that as my parents insisted that I should be home-schooled. I begged and begged to go to school and eventually they gave in.

We moved after I'd only been there for a month. It crushed me but I promptly asked to go to school again.

"We have to get settled first, then you can go," my mom told me.

I remember the conversation clearly. "I don't wanna wait. I want to go to school tomorrow."

"Tomorrow's Saturday," my mom had said patiently.

"Then I want to go to school on Monday."

"We'll see what happens." She set down a snack and put one of my favorite science kid shows on to keep me entertained while she went to unpack.

* * *

IN THE MIDDLE of second grade I came home to find my mom in the kitchen putting some things into a small box. We'd just made a cool project in art and I rushed in to show her.

"Look what I made!" I held up the mess of glue, construction paper and glitter.

My mom didn't look up. "Go pack your clothes."

"But, Mom, look!"

She slammed a plate down so hard that it cracked and I jumped. "I said go pack."

"Why?"

"Your dad got a new job and we have to go."

I started to cry. "I don't want to go!" My new friend invited me to her birthday party over the weekend.

Forgetting the broken plate my mom hugged me. She helped me to my room.

"When your dad gets home tonight we'll get ice cream before we go. How's that sound?"

I continued to cry but the promise of the sweet treat soothed me some. My mom left me to pack. Naturally, my few toys went into my bag first.

* * *

"DADDY, CAN I ASK YOU A QUESTION?" I climbed down the stairs to the basement of the house we were living in. We'd only been there a few weeks. Because it was so close to the end of third grade my parents had said I would be homeschooled again and go back to school in the fall.

"Sure, peanut." My dad tossed a cover sheet over the workbench he'd had set up and it covered all the tools he had there. I didn't understand what all the tools were for since I never saw him actually working on anything.

"Am I adopted?"

My dad didn't answer right away. He always had a measured way of approaching things. His temper was much calmer than my mom's so I tended to go to him with the Big Questions. He sat down on a stool and pulled me onto his lap.

"What do you think it would mean if you were adopted?"

I thought the question over like I imagined my dad would. I liked the way he asked me what I thought. It made me feel grown up in a way I didn't get from my mom. "I think… I think it means you and mom picked me. And I think it means I have two moms and dads!" That thought was exciting. We moved so often I had few friends and certainly none that lasted. And I had no cousins or other family like I knew the other kids at school had. I still wished for a little brother or sister.

Dad laughed slightly. "Well, you're right on both things. And, yes, your mom and I picked you out when you were a baby. Out of all the babies we could have chosen we picked you."

That made me smile and I felt a warm spot spread from my chest.

We then spent a few minutes comparing our differences. How both my parents had blond hair and I had black hair that was tight with curls. My skin was naturally a few shades darker brown. He explained that made me lucky because my mom would turn bright red after just a few minutes in the sun but I just tanned every summer.

"Can I meet my other mom and dad one day?" I was thrilled by the prospect of another set of parents. If one set of parents was nice, how much better would it be to have two? And maybe I'd have more family. Maybe even some kids my own age.

My dad's expression went serious. "No. That's not possible."

"Why?" My heart broke at the idea of all the lost family I'd imagined even if for a brief moment.

"Because your other mom and dad didn't want to take care of you. That's why they gave you to us. So we could take care of you and love you for them."

His words stung but I didn't have the right words to express it. "Oh."

My dad kissed the top of my head and gently set me down off his lap. "You'll always have us. Now go see your mom, I have to finish with this project."

I desperately wanted to ask what the project was but I knew better. It was one of the things I wasn't allowed to question. I also knew when I was being dismissed so I made my way back upstairs and to my room.

* * *

BY THE TIME I entered high school I'd lost count of the number of schools I'd attended. I ended up homeschooled for the better part of my middle school years.

I'd stopped questioning all the moving we did and just accepted it as a fact of life. It became easier to constantly be the new kid. I found it more frustrating to always end up in remedial classes. My grades were always good and even though my parents were fairly relaxed in their homeschooling methods I soaked up knowledge seemingly faster than they could get it to me.

By my junior year of high school I started to make plans on how to get my GED and get into college. College was exciting because it meant my parents could move if they needed to but I didn't have to. I could stay on campus or in a nearby apartment and could finally focus on school the way I wanted to.

I felt good about the place we lived in currently. The school was nice, smaller than most I went to and I'd actually made a few friends. I knew it was temporary but it was nice anyway.

The group of kids I spoke to all liked to compare various TV shows they streamed. They would recommend shows to each other and although I'd never been a big TV watcher for the most part I started trying a few of the shows they suggested.

Most didn't hold my interest but there was one documentary series that I found interesting that they all talked about.

It was a series on serial killers. Most of them had been caught years ago but every so often an episode would end with a note that the murders were unsolved and police were still accepting information.

Those were the episodes that got talked about the most at school. We all enjoyed the mystery of it, but I also thought it was a bit morbid.

I'd decided I would only watch until the end of the first season and then would drop it. We were likely to move again soon anyway.

As I started the last episode I pulled out some homework I had to work on. I only vaguely listened as the narrator started talking about a family of four.

I heard something about them being immigrants from Mexico and looked up long enough to see an old family photo. The mother held a baby in her arms and there was a little girl of about three holding the father's hand. With her dark curly hair she reminded me of some of my old photos. Not that my parents kept many of those.

One of the detectives interviewed for the show talked about the murder. I tuned most of that out but heard how another detective who had started working on the cold case tied the murders to another few murders in another county. He went on to say that they'd never found the body of the baby but because the family were all immigrants he suspected it hadn't been investigated as fully as it should have been.

I looked up and listened as they showed another picture of the family. I realized that the murders had only happened about sixteen years ago. That unsettled me for some reason.

Then the detective talked about the other murders and how he felt certain the killers were still out there and had likely committed others.

They talked about some of the other information that had been pieced together once the second detective tied the murder of the family to a few others in the state.

Someone had come forward and insisted they saw one of the victims with a couple before they died.

The show then posted two sketches. I stared. The faces were familiar. Too familiar.

A man and woman.

Before I could talk myself out of it I heard the front door open.

It was my parents. I scrambled to turn the TV off. As I did I took one last look at the sketches.

My parents.

They called from downstairs. "Hurry up and come down. We brought dinner back. Just something fast. Your father got another new job so we'll start packing after dinner."

PLAY WITH ME, PART 2

I hadn't been home since I left for college. I'd stayed on or near campus over the summers but now that I was graduating I returned to the house to pack some things with the intention of never returning.

My parents, on the other hand, had made it pretty clear they were staying in the area and would stay in the area for the rest of their lives.

I couldn't.

"You sure you don't want me to come in with you, Rocio?" My girlfriend from college had come with me. We'd met my first year there and I hadn't told her anything about what happened to Mariana until a few months ago. As far as she had known I was an only child. But when I told her that I wasn't and that my little brother had died in an accident when I was a kid and my sister went missing before I started college she was so understanding about it I'd almost been suspicious. Of course, I hadn't told her what had really happened the night Mariana disappeared. I'd tried explaining it to our parents and the police. When they insisted I'd been doing drugs or maybe even made the whole story up I stopped talking about it.

"I'm sure. I'm just packing a box with a few things. They probably already got rid of everything else." I spoke to my parents on holidays and birthdays but it was strained now.

As I walked up to the front door I saw a note. It simply said they had something come up and that I should feel free to take what items of mine I wanted. Anything else would be tossed by the end of the week. I wasn't exactly surprised so I just adjusted the box I'd brought with me and went inside.

* * *

Lupita and I stayed at a motel that night. We were going to drive back to school in the morning, attend graduation at the end of the week and then look for an apartment together.

I couldn't sleep that night, though, and she slipped out of bed to join me as I stared out the window of the motel.

"I'm going to go out for a while," I told her.

"I can come with you."

My stomach went cold at that and I shook my head. "No, better not."

"Where are you going?" She still had her arms around my waist. She felt warm against my back but I was shivering slightly.

"I'll be back by the morning. Just stay here. Please." I couldn't stomach the thought of losing her too.

"Rocio, you're scaring me."

I turned in her arms so I could give her a quick kiss. "I'll be back," I promised.

I grabbed my jacket and left the motel. I didn't want to take the car even though I knew Lupita wouldn't mind if I did. But I didn't want to leave her stranded if something happened.

I pulled the jacket close and walked to the woods.

When I got there an hour later I was surprised to see a car sitting just outside the woods.

"What the hell are you doing here?"

Lupita was lounging on the hood of the car and pretended to look surprised when she heard me. "Did you know most newspaper articles are online these days? Even local ones."

I scowled but went over to stand next to her at the car. "Obviously."

"A lot of people think these woods are haunted."

I tensed and tried not to be overwhelmed by memories of my last time in those woods. "I don't believe in ghosts."

"Then what are you doing here?"

I didn't know what to say to that. I just knew that I had to get in there.

"Let me come with you." Lupita slid off the car and took my hand.

I didn't know how to tell her how much that idea terrified me. I could still see the last time I saw Mariana or the form of my little brother.

"Let me come," she said again.

"I don't know what happened to her. I have to know what happened to her," I said quietly.

Lupita nodded and took my hand. I took a shaky breath and gripped her hand tightly as we headed into the woods.

We wandered for an hour. I think Lupita thought we were just going without any particular destination in mind. But I knew where we were going.

"Do you want to talk about what happened?" Lupita kept her voice down but it still felt a little too loud.

A part of me wanted to. But I was also somehow afraid that I might summon up whatever had taken Mariana. I shook my head.

Lupita didn't push it. "I read a little bit about the other disappearances."

"These woods are surprisingly big. People get lost, die of exposure..."

"There's a lot of ghost stories about this place."

I scowled. "I don't believe in ghosts."

If Lupita thought anything of me insisting on repeating myself she didn't say anything of it. "People can't really agree on it, though. Some say it could just be restless spirits that lure people off. Others that these woods used to be part of some bigger burial ground and that's why there's so much activity."

I thought of the shadowy form that had spoken with my little brother's voice.

"My little brother was only four when he died," I said softly.

Lupita was quiet for a moment. "What happened to him?"

I tightened my grip on her hand. So far we'd been making do with the lights from our phones as flashlights. "Mariana and I were a couple years older so we had a hard time playing with him sometimes. She was ten and I was twelve and he really wanted to go bike riding with us. He thought we were so cool because we could ride bikes without training wheels and he was still on his little kid tricycle. But Mariana and I were doing something else so Mari told him to go ahead and we'd catch up. I don't… I don't think either of us really thought about it. He wandered off and…and we thought he'd stay in the yard. He wasn't supposed to go off the driveway without us but he did and…" I cut off for a moment and shivered. It wasn't cold but the hair on the back of my neck was standing on end anyway. "He got hit by a car. It was an accident but it took Mari a while to get past it. I think she still blamed herself sometimes."

"That's awful." Lupita squeezed my hand and I was grateful for her presence.

I wanted to tell her that I thought I'd seen him that night. The wind picked up before I could.

"You feel that?" she asked me quietly. She shone her light around but all I saw were the trees.

"Yeah," I breathed. Something was here. Even if we couldn't see it. Our lights seemed dimmer and it was so dark I felt like it was pressing down on me and made it hard to breathe.

"You know," Lupita started, voice quiet, "someone online said they had a theory about this place. They said everyone that had gone missing had also lost someone they were close to. They thought it might have something to do…"

She cut off as the wind started blowing so harshly we both ducked and tried to cover our faces with one arm as twigs and dry leaves pelted us in the face.

I heard a voice through the wind but it was indistinct. But I knew the sound.

"Mari!" I tugged to free my hand but Lupita but she held firm.

"Rocio! No! It's not her!"

I didn't care. I had to see her. I had to let her know how sorry I was. She had to know that I hadn't forgiven myself. That I would have given anything to be the one to go with Hector instead of her.

"Let go!" I tried to tug again and this time our hands came apart. I fell to the side and my phone cracked, the light going out. I looked back to try and see Lupita but the whirlwind had picked up between us and I couldn't see her through the dark and the swirling leaves.

I heard Mari's voice again and it was stronger this time. I got to my feet and ran that way.

I kept going until I tripped over a branch and hit the ground so hard that lights flashed in my vision. I took a moment to roll onto my back and blink to focus again.

The temperature dropped fast and I saw a shadow formed next to me. I expected it to be small and short like Hector. This time the shadow was taller and seemed to have longer hair.

"Rocio." It was Mari's voice.

I didn't move but I felt my heart sink.

"Why did you leave me?"

I swallowed hard and stared at the shadow. "I'm sorry," I managed around the lump in my throat. I was shaking hard.

"Come with us."

"I can't," I said quietly. I couldn't help but think of Lupita waiting for me.

"You left me. You left *us*."

Guilt twisted my gut. "No, I didn't. I didn't mean to!"

The shadow shifted closer. "Come with us. You owe us."

I shook my head slightly. I rubbed my eyes hard with my hands. "I'm sorry."

The wind picked up again and I heard footsteps. I didn't dare look up, though.

"Rocio!" It was Lupita's voice. "Don't! It's the guilt! They feed off…"

The wind kicked up again and Lupita's voice was lost to the gust.

I heard Mari's voice again but I didn't register the words. I was thinking about what Lupita said. It slowly started to make sense.

"Mari, I can't. I'm not…it wasn't my fault. It *wasn't*." I believed that. For the most part. It was natural to feel guilt, wasn't it? My siblings had both died or disappeared.

The shadow elongated and started screeching so loudly my ears popped. I curled up and covered my ears.

The wind picked up even more until I thought I might just get blown away. The twigs and leaves picked up so badly it actually started to hurt.

Just when I started to think that the screeching would actually start to make my ears bleed it all suddenly stopped.

My ears were ringing and I didn't dare move for a moment. Then someone nudged my shoulder and I blinked.

Lupita leaned over me. "Are you okay?"

I nodded shakily and she helped me sit up. I could see the sky starting to lighten.

"You did it." She threw her arms around me and hugged me tightly.

I clung to her tightly. We stayed there for a while until we could finally see and then made our way back to the car.

"Do you think that's it?" I asked quietly.

Lupita turned to me and nodded. "Yes. I think. I think whatever those things were they weren't your siblings. Not really. Your siblings, their spirits, would want you to be happy. Whatever that was? I'm pretty sure it wasn't them. Not really."

I thought that over and reached out to take her hand. "I knew I wanted to stay with you."

She smiled and squeezed my hand. "Let's get out of here, huh?"

I nodded and she turned the car on so we could head back to our new home. This time I knew I wouldn't be back here and I was fine with that.

WILDLIFE REFUGE

When we imagined an alien invasion no one ever imagined that our greatest asset would be the planet itself. As most of the human population disappeared into holding areas that the aliens set up it was left up to the people who were still free to try and fight back.

Sure the militias, and anyone with a gun, no sense and a large plot of land thought they could go all Rambo on the invaders. And a few tried. But it was the people like myself who had no guns and just enough knowledge on how to live off the land who started to notice something interesting.

As the aliens slowly started to expand out from the cities from which they started their invasion not only did it become harder for them to find humans but they started to run into more and more wildlife.

In an effort to help other survivors I've collected what first-hand accounts of the encounters I could.

Africa:

I think it started as a joke. Some smartass managed to get across to the aliens, who seemed to understand us better than we understood them, that when looking for escaped humans the best thing they could do would be to check rivers or any other bodies of water they could find. The bigger the better.

Up until that point the aliens had seen the local wildlife, a few lions and giraffes and more wildebeest than they knew what to do with but had barely paid any attention to them.

A group of them went out to search for anyone hidden in the brush. About half a dozen went out. Two came back.

The thing about the aliens was they were shorter than the average human but because of their multiple legs that made them look like some kind of weird centaur and bug hybrid so when they moved they could go quite quickly when they wanted to. Certainly faster than most humans and it had been their advantage so far.

Even though we couldn't understand them we could see that the remaining two were agitated. They conversed with some of the other aliens and then came to the pen where a group of us were being held.

"River," one of the aliens said using a system they'd rigged to recreate human speech in a way we could understand. "Creatures in the river."

A few of the others with me backed away and didn't want to get involved. I stepped forward.

"Which creature?"

The aliens gestured and clicked amongst themselves for a moment.

"Large. Many teeth," the alien said.

"Crocodile? They eat just about anything."

The aliens consulted for another moment. "Did not eat. Very large. Round."

I almost laughed but I held it back and grinned instead. "Hippo. Very dangerous."

The aliens turned to each other. The two survivors seemed to want out of this conversation but the others kept them hedged in.

"Fight? Defense?"

I shrugged. "Hippos have no weaknesses."

They clicked back and forth in their own language for another moment before leaving.

The next day another team went out. This time only one returned and we could hear them going back and forth about what happened. Slowly we started to recognize they now had a word for hippo.

Within a week their numbers had decreased noticeably. They tried asking for other ways to find the surviving humans. Our answer was always the same: check the rivers and watering holes. We started making plans for escape knowing that it was obvious if we could get out of the area that we would be able to survive on the land far easier than the aliens who continued to have fatal encounters with the local wildlife.

ALASKA:

We thought the cold might offer us some protection from the aliens. Turned out they were well enough equipped for space and that meant being able to tolerate the cold about as well as we could with the proper equipment.

My family and I managed to stay ahead of them for quite a while. I saw an encounter where a group of the aliens came across a polar bear. The bear was probably hungry but it gave the aliens a wide berth. They didn't seem particularly bothered with it either. I was keeping an eye out for anything we could use against the aliens but they seemed pretty hardy so far.

I was spying on one of their camps and considering the best way to sabotage it when a new animal they hadn't encountered yet came seemingly out of nowhere.

It was smaller than the aliens and at first I thought it was a bear cub. I had hopes that if it was then the mother might come and disrupt their camp. Don't mess with a mama bear, right?

I was mistaken. As I watched I realized a wolverine had come across their camp. The aliens didn't seem concerned about the creature because of its size.

A few scuttled towards it, leaning in to investigate.

From a distance I couldn't be entirely sure what happened or what set it off but the next thing I knew the wolverine was on top of one of the aliens. There were spurts of dark liquid and panicked clicking sounds. One of the aliens tried to help the one under attack but the wolverine turned on it.

The only thing that kept me from running off was the fact I didn't want to distract the wolverine. And a small part of me knew this would be important in the future.

Within a few minutes the entire alien camp was dead or severely injured.

The wolverine didn't seem interested in eating the aliens and once it was done it wandered back off into the wilderness. I waited for a while before I dared leave to go back to my family. I'd never seen anything like that before but I had heard stories of wolverines that were brave enough to attack humans.

As I left the camp I started trying to think of ways to encourage the wolverines in the area to target the aliens. I had a feeling, though, that with no aliens left alive to tell about that particular danger that it would be quite a while before they realized what the real killer out here was and hopefully even longer before they figured out a way to fight back.

HELPING HANDS

The thing about growing up with any kind of health condition that alters the way you live your life is that you learn to live with it. You learn what is going to be a bad day and what will be a good day and if you're lucky, the routine becomes normal enough that you hardly even think about it anymore. Anyone who's able-bodied or 'normal' tends to make a big deal about it and sometimes they feel bad for you and sometimes they want you to just suck it up and stop talking about your disease or illness or whatever so that they don't feel inconvenienced by it.

In my case, growing up meant taking certain precautions every month to ensure my safety and the safety of others around me. Luckily being born with lycanthropy meant that I have better control over myself when I transform than others might. Plus, I figured out pretty early on that if I ate a ton of protein before I transformed that the whole starving werewolf thing wouldn't be an issue.

See, everyone assumes werewolves are bloodthirsty and starving all the time but really it's mostly just the fact that the transformation takes an incredible amount of energy. I mean that physically. The solution? Eat a ton of calories, preferably protein and the like, and when you wake up your wolf form isn't quite so starving and blood-thirsty.

Now, like I said, this is a pretty normal thing for me. Every month since I was a kid I transform and even in my middle of nowhere school I've been able to keep it quiet. Anything weird happens and the locals are happy to blame it on coyotes.

Then I woke up from one of my transformations and staring me down was the lifeless form of one of the seniors from my high school. His chest was clawed open and there was blood covering the grass all around him. I screamed and only barely remembered to collect my clothes from where I'd changed out of them next to the lake before I ran to my car and drove myself home.

* * *

UNDERSTANDABLY, once the body was found things got a little tense at school. The police came and talked to a bunch of different kids from school to find out what the guy had been up to and if they knew where he'd been.

I already had an idea what had happened. It was pretty obvious for anyone who had ever seen a werewolf attack. There weren't any other animals in the area that could have done it. I couldn't exactly go to the police about that, though. And I knew it wasn't me. I hadn't been covered in blood. Plus, even though my memories of my transformation were never that clear I knew enough to know it hadn't been me. I would have remembered hunting anything. My trick of eating my weight in food before I turned hadn't failed me yet in over a decade of transformations.

That meant that there was another werewolf in the area. And I had to find out who it was. If they knew what they were and still attacked humans? Well, then I'd have to work that out. But if they didn't know and were new to the whole transformation process? I had to help them.

* * *

WE HAD JUST HAD a new kid move in a few weeks ago so she was obviously my first suspect. I walked right up to her when I saw her at her locker.

"Hi. My name's Riley. You're new, right? Amanda?"

She blinked at me in surprise. "Uh, yeah. We have pre-calc together."

I beamed. I got butterflies in my stomach when she looked at me. Her light blue shirt really brought out the color of her eyes. It matched perfectly. I also felt a bit stupid since that wasn't something I'd ever paid attention to before. "Yeah, we do. Hey, do you want to get lunch with me? I have a car. We could get something off campus. If you wanted." I had no problem being forward usually. But I found myself feeling nervous. I wanted her to say yes and not just so I could figure out if she was the new werewolf in the area.

"Oh." Amanda stared at me for a moment and then nodded slowly. "Yeah, um, I guess so."

"Great!" Those damn butterflies in my stomach just wouldn't go away. If anything they brought some friends to play in my gut. "Meet me in front by the main office? I'll drive over and pick you up. It's an older Camry."

"Okay. Sure. Thanks," she said and I bolted down the hallway before the butterflies could stage a revolt or something.

* * *

LUNCH WAS GREAT. Or, I mean, spending the time with Amanda was great. The butterflies refused to settle long enough for me to do more than pick at my food.

"You like it here?" I asked her.

She shrugged. We'd just gone to a chain burger place and she picked at the salad she'd gotten.

I still had another night of transformations so I had gotten two burger meals and had just about inhaled the first one and was unwrapping the second as she stared at her salad.

"It's not too bad," she said.

I could feel her staring at my meal. It didn't bother me, it was why I usually didn't eat with anyone, though. "Sorry, my period. You're not vegetarian, are you?"

She laughed. "No, just… trying to be healthier."

"I think you're gorgeous," I blurted. I knew what it meant when girls said they were trying to be 'healthier'. Usually it meant one too many guys or even other girls had made some unkind passing comments. Or maybe even been flat out rude. But even I was not usually that forward.

She went bright red.

"Sorry. I don't have a great filter." It wasn't completely untrue but something about her had completely destroyed mine.

She smiled faintly. "It's okay. You're nice."

I felt myself redden slightly and I took a giant bite of my burger to cover it. "What made you move out here?"

"My dad got a job here."

"Oh, okay. Cool. My moms both work for the town."

She nodded and didn't even blink at the news. It was nice.

"Have you seen anything weird in the woods?" I blurted.

She glanced at me and shook her head. "I don't go out after dark."

"Cool. Any reason?"

She shrugged. "No real reason to. You know, homework and stuff. And not a lot of friends."

"I'd like to be your friend." I really needed to get myself under control.

She smiled a little and my stomach felt like I'd just dropped off a rollercoaster. "Are you always like this?

"No. Well. Yes. Kind of."

"It's nice." She put her salad aside and reached for one of the fries in the container next to my leg.

I smiled back and knew I was going to be in trouble. I'd never had a crush on another girl before.

* * *

I WANTED to try and find the other werewolf by that night. Or else someone else could be in danger. Which also put me in danger by extension. But if I could get to them and warn them about what was going on then the next day we could talk it over and I could help them. It might be nice to not have to hide my secret for once.

But by the end of the day I was convinced Amanda wasn't the one I was looking for. Well, she was, but not in that way. That left me back at square one by the end of school but I had to finish my homework and get ready for my transformation.

I took so long getting ready that I had to pack up my dinner for the transformation and start eating it in the car on the way to the woods. I parked at a different spot and made my way towards the lake. I'd brought some extra burgers and some medium rare steaks in case I ran into the other werewolf.

The moon was just starting to peek out as I shed my clothes and tucked them away so I could find them in the morning. I peered out through the trees towards the lake.

As I felt the transformation start I saw someone stagger towards the edge of the lake. I panicked and thought it had to be some kids from school but no one else followed the person out. As I watched I realized that the other person was going through their transformation.

That would have been great if I hadn't already started mine as well. I could at least control myself to a certain degree and as my bones started to grind together and grow I started towards the lake.

It was pretty obvious that whoever it was was trying to get as far out into the lake as they could before fully transforming. I couldn't sort out why as I made myself focus on one thing. I had to get to them and pull them back.

Things started to go fuzzy at that point. I was vaguely aware of half swimming and half drowning my way to the other werewolf. The last thing I remember before completing the transformation was the brightest blue eyes I'd ever seen in my life.

* * *

AMANDA. My eyes flew open. I scanned the area near me and this time the person near me was very much alive. She was curled up a few feet away from me and her arms and legs were covered in freshly healed scratches. Her side had some newly scarred deeper cuts and I assumed that had to be the wound that had turned her.

I didn't dare leave to get my clothes in case she woke up before I got back.

She stirred a moment later and I quickly closed my eyes and held up a hand. "Easy, it's me. You're naked, but it's cool, I'm not looking." I was probably red head to toe.

She made a startled sound and I heard the grass rustle as she scrambled away. "What's going on?"

"Uh, well, you're a werewolf."

She didn't say anything and I cracked an eye open to check if she was still there.

"Don't look!"

I closed my eyes again promptly. "There's a blanket and some clothes a few yards that way. Clothes are mine but you can borrow them."

I heard her move away and a moment later my clothes hit me in the face. I peeked and saw she'd wrapped herself up in the blanket. I quickly pulled the clothes on.

"C'mon, I'll take you to my place and we can talk."

Amanda hesitated. "Won't your moms wonder?"

"Nah. They know all about me. Werewolf lesbian and all."

Amanda stared at me and I made a note that I really needed to watch what I said.

* * *

"SO I'M A WEREWOLF."

I nodded. I'd gotten Amanda back to my house. Luckily for us both it was a Saturday and she said her parents wouldn't notice her missing. They hadn't the other two days.

"I'd... I'd kind of suspected," she admitted. "Did some research. I read that werewolves can't swim."

It was my turn to stare at her. "You were going to drown yourself?"

She nodded without looking up at me.

I slowly made my way over and sat next to her. "Amanda... it may seem like it sucks but it's manageable. Trust me. I've been doing this since I was a kid."

She was trembling but that seemed to startle her because she met my gaze finally. "A kid? Your moms know?"

"Of course. They've helped me work it out. That's why we live here."

Amanda was quiet. "I think I killed that boy."

I wasn't going to lie to her. "Probably. But we can work it out. I promise."

"How? How am I supposed to live with that?"

I made sure to pick my words carefully. "I can help you. I know of resources. This wouldn't be the first accident. And yes, it's awful, but I can help you." I took her hand and she didn't pull back.

"I don't know," she said softly.

I didn't let go of her hand. "Let me help you. Because the lake? That's not the answer."

I wasn't sure how long we sat there together but she slowly rested her head on my shoulder.

"Ok," she said finally, just as I started to think that maybe she'd fallen asleep. "I'll let you help me."

I felt a weight immediately slide off my shoulders. I squeezed her hand. "Good. It's not so bad," I promised.

FRIENDLY CHAT, PART 2

Being at home with Jamie didn't go quite as well as I had thought. Well, admittedly, I hadn't thought it through much. I just thought that having her there with me for the winter break would make everything easier. It had while I'd been at college.

But at home things were different. At college I stopped seeing my friends.

My parents wouldn't leave me alone. My mom's favorite question was, "Are you okay?" in this sickening tone. Like she thought I was going to break if she asked too forcefully. Or if she didn't ask that I might do something crazy.

I had opted to spend as much time in my room as possible. I lay in bed with the blinds closed and the lights off. A little bit of light from outside just came from the edges and I could just make out Jaime's form on the bed in front of me.

"Your mom made breakfast," she said.

I shook my head. "I'm not hungry."

"I didn't think so. But thought you'd want to know anyway."

The only thing I wanted was to stay right where I was. With Jaime. "Doesn't matter. I hate going down there."

"Why?"

It was all I could do to keep myself from reaching out and pushing some hair back from Jaime's face. "She asks so many questions."

Jaime nodded in understanding. "So don't. Stay here. With me."

I reached for her and put my hand on the bed between us. She lightly placed her hand by mine and it felt a bit like I'd stuck my hand into a bowl of ice water. The feeling slowly spread up my arm.

"I wish we could go back to school already."

"Well. You don't have to. What difference does it make if you're here or at school? I'm with you either way."

I had to admit she had a point. I closed my eyes, my whole arm numb, but it was the only way I could feel close to her. It was the afternoon but I felt myself fall asleep.

* * *

MOST OF MY break started to blend together. I slept during the day so I could be awake at night to talk with Jaime. That was when she was strongest and I could go and get a snack without my parents giving me a hard time.

At some point down the line I'd stopped charging my phone. It lay dead under my bed or maybe until the pile of clothes that was spread across my room.

I roused myself slightly as someone knocked at my door.

"Jenna, open up."

I was surprised it wasn't my mom's voice.

"Bri?" I rolled out of bed and opened the door. I was still surprised to see my friend there. We'd been close in high school but I hadn't really heard from her a while.

"Your mom told me what happened. Get dressed, we're going out."

"What time is it?" I squinted and tried to look around but I'd unplugged my desk clock at some point.

"It's like ten at night. Get dressed, you have ten minutes. I'll wait downstairs." She grinned quickly and turned to go downstairs.

I wanted to argue with her but she disappeared down the stairs before I could.

I turned back into my room and felt my shoulder down to my fingers go numb as Jaime put a hand there.

"You're not going out, are you? It's late."

I rubbed at my eyes and shrugged. "Be rude not to go." I changed and managed to find some clear clothes. "Besides, aren't you going to come?"

"I'd better not."

By the time I'd pulled a fresh t-shirt over my head she was gone. I blinked around my room and felt a nervous pit settle in my stomach. The thought of staying home tugged at me. It was more time with Jaime.

"C'mon, let's go!" Bri called from downstairs.

I grabbed a jacket from my floor and pulled it on, suddenly aware of how cold I was. Then I went to meet Bri downstairs.

* * *

WE DIDN'T TALK for a while. She drove us to get snacks at the local convenience store that was still open and then we parked at an empty lot by the high school.

It wasn't long before I started feeling antsy and looked around for Jaime. Why wasn't she here? What if she didn't come back?

"Waiting for someone?" Bri asked, noticing my gaze.

"Jaime," I blurted.

"Your girlfriend?"

I regretted saying anything but I nodded.

"You mean like a ghost or like you just wish she was here?"

I hesitated. "Ghost. We've... been talking."

"Oh. Huh. How's that work?"

"Well," I started, "I'm not real sure. I just started talking to her one day and then it's like the more I did the more I could hear her and now she's almost always there. She's stronger at night." I didn't care if Bri thought I was crazy. It felt good to say it.

"But she's not here now?" Bri looked around like she thought she might actually see her.

"No. She didn't want me to come out. Night's been our time. We talk in bed and stuff."

"You stay up all night now? Is that why your mom said she doesn't see you and you don't even come out to eat anymore?"

I shrugged. "I guess so. I just… don't feel hungry. When I'm with Jaime…" I didn't know how to explain it but I pulled my jacket tighter around myself. I felt cold from the inside out.

Bri twisted in her seat so she could look at me. We hadn't gotten out of the car but she left it running so the heat was on. I knew it had to be comfortable because she'd tossed her coat in the backseat. "Jenna, you need to take care of yourself. Jaime would want you to do that. Real Jaime. Not ghost Jaime."

"I am taking care of myself," I said defensively. "What do you know anyway?"

Bri didn't seem hurt by my tone and I realized I was grateful for that. I hadn't meant to sound so short with her. "I know that spending more time talking to the dead than the living can't last. Trust me. Jaime's gone and it sucks but you need to start figuring out how to live your life."

I shook my head and panic rose in my chest. "No. I'm, I'm doing fine. School is fine, everything's fine, I can do this. I need her with me."

Bri put a hand on my leg. I flinched. Her hand was warm even through my jeans. Slowly that warmth spread through me and I only just then started to realize how bone cold I felt.

"Jenna, I know we don't talk a lot anymore, but maybe that's good. Maybe you need to hear this from someone who isn't so close to you. I think it's time to let Jaime go."

I didn't know what to say to that. The idea seemed incomprehensible but a small part of me clung to that. After all, wasn't moving on what people were supposed to do when they lost someone? How long could Jaime last anyway?

All those thoughts got tangled in my head. We didn't say anything after that. Finally, around midnight, after we'd finished our snacks, Bri drove me back home.

* * *

FOR THE NEXT week Bri continued to come over. She came over earlier and earlier until after a week we were outside when it was actually light out.

"I think Jaime's starting to really hate me being out all the time," I said.

Bri was quiet. We'd gotten hot chocolate. I was starting to feel warmer in general but something in my core still felt numb and cold. "Are you sure it's a good idea to keep talking to her?"

"What? How can you even say that?"

"Jenna, I'm worried about you. All you do is talk about Jaime. You hardly eat and you sleep all day except when you're talking to her. I'm just…worried."

I scowled down at my hot chocolate cup. "I don't want to let her go. I just, I just got her back!"

Bri put a hand on my leg and again I was shocked by how good it felt. I'd gotten so used to Jaime's cold touch. But this reminded me how nice it was to be with someone who was actually alive. "She's not back. She's…lingering. And maybe she's only doing so because you keep talking to her."

I refused to look up from my Styrofoam cup. "No. No, she came back. To talk to me."

Bri gave me such a sympathetic look I had the urge to slap her. "Did she come back or did you bring her back?"

That made me stop. I'd ached so hard for Jaime that I hadn't thought of it that way. Sure, I'd been encouraged to talk to her as a form of grieving but had that called her back somehow? "I don't know. I don't know how any of this works." I didn't say that I thought I'd worried I was going crazy at first. Maybe I had been.

"Let her go, Jenna. Figure out how to honor her and start living your life again. You can't keep this up."

I felt tears welling up in my eyes. "I don't…If I go back to school she's still going to be there. She's everywhere." If I had called her back I knew that as part had been easy.

"Maybe you should take some time off. You could stay here. I'm still local. We could hang out. You could get a job and then figure out what to do from there."

"I don't know what my parents will say to that."

Bri shrugged. "Who cares. You need to do what's best for you. That's what's important."

I nodded slowly.

* * *

I DIDN'T SEE Jaime again until the next night. I was sitting on the edge of my bed when I felt the room go cold. The usual sign that Jaime had appeared.

Neither of us said anything for a long moment so I took a deep breath.

"Bri says I need to let you go." I couldn't look at her.

"I don't want to leave you," Jaime said softly.

I tried to swallow the lump in my throat. "And I don't want to let you go but. But we can't keep doing this."

Jaime put a hand on my arm and for the first time I shuddered. She pulled her hand back. When I looked up at her she was thinner, more transparent than she had been in months.

"I love you, Jaime, but I…"

"I know. I've known for a while, I think."

My heart ached.

"It's okay, Jenna. You'll be okay."

"What about you?"

She smiled slightly but didn't answer. I couldn't take it anymore and I started sobbing. A little while later, I sat up and looked around. She was gone. My room had returned to a normal temperature. Even the deep core cold I'd felt for months felt broken up.

I reached for my phone. I texted Bri to ask if she wanted to hang out.

FINAL SCENE (FROM AN UNMADE HORROR MOVIE)

my's heart pounded so loudly she felt sure that would be the thing to give her away. She held her breath to do everything she could to keep quiet but that just made her head feel like it was going to explode with every heartbeat. She strained to hear but doubted anything would give the creature away. So far it had managed to move silently over the dry leaves outside and over the creaky floorboards of the old house despite the long black robes it wore.

Something outside the closet where Amy hid rustled and her eyes went wide. It didn't help; outside the closet was just as dark as it was inside. The generator the house ran on had been damaged hours ago. Her muscles were tense with fear, but also with the impulse to run. She had to find Jo. She was still alive, Amy was sure of it.

Something shifted and then it felt like the pressure on Amy's lungs vanished. She let out a slow breath to give her lungs a chance to recover. Slowly she got back to her feet and counted to five.

One.

She took another slow breath and listened hard but she could just tell the creature wasn't there.

Two.

She reached for the closet doorknob with one shaking hand.

Three.

Her stomach turned but she didn't fight it.

Four.

She willed her breathing to steady. Her heart still pounded painfully but she ignored it now.

Five.

Amy pushed the door open. The last time she'd seen Jo the other girl ran for the basement. They'd been running from the creature and she'd meant for them to stay together but fear had been driving them both and they'd gone separate ways: Jo to the basement and Amy further into the house until she hit the closet she'd hid in.

She made her way down the stairs, hating every creak of the old wooden steps as she did. Amy kept one hand on the wall to guide herself. At least upstairs there was moonlight coming through the windows and a few hallways in the main house had those energy saver nightlights that only came on during power outages. In the basement there was nothing and Amy felt herself blinking automatically to try and make her eyes adjust.

"Jo?" Her voice came out hoarse and even though she was whispering it still sounded too loud. "Jo, it's me." The thought that the creature may have already killed her popped into Amy's mind and she tried to shove it away. Jo would be alive, she had to be.

Amy made her way further into the basement but didn't move her hand from the wall. She imagined the cobwebs or insects she might run into and that made her skin crawl just as much as the thought of the creature upstairs.

Somewhere to her right the gravel and dirt floor shifted and Amy tensed. She turned automatically and strained to see into the black. Something brushed against her arm and she jumped. As she tried to scramble back something warm grabbed her arm.

"It's me," Jo hissed in her ear.

Amy's stomach lurched with fear but the wave of relief at hearing Jo's voice quelled it. "Jo!" She wanted to hug her but they weren't that close. Amy still wasn't quite sure how she'd managed to get invited to the weekend at the house. Jo mostly kept to herself and her small group of friends. Amy was more outgoing and had spoken to Jo a handful of times in their classes or said hello to her in the hall. As much as Amy had wanted to be a better friend to the other girl it seemed like Jo had always been perfectly content with her small group of friends and had no time for anyone else.

"I have an idea," Jo whispered into Amy's ear. She had to tip toe to do so and Amy leaned in a little to get close. "My parents keep spare gas cans in the garage for the lawn mower."

Amy made a little strangled noise of surprise. "And get ourselves blown up in the process?"

"Do you have a better idea?"

Amy stayed quiet. Admittedly she didn't. Their cell phones had each gone missing throughout the day and as soon as the sun had gone down they'd found the pile of charred electronics on the front porch of the house. They'd all thought that someone in the house was playing a joke on them or that maybe Jo was trying to make a point by inviting them to the middle of nowhere and taking the phones when she thought they were too reliant on the technology.

"I didn't think so," Jo whispered. She didn't let go of Amy's arm but gently turned her so they could head back up the stairs.

Amy let Jo take the lead. It was her family's house after all, but she also felt better having her there.

The two made their way as quietly as they could through the house. Jo took them the long way to the back porch exit. If they had cut through the living room they would have had to go by Kim's bloodied body. Kim, with deep claw marks across her neck and chest. Amy felt sick thinking about it and she unconsciously reached for Jo's hand.

Surprisingly Jo didn't pull away or even comment. She just laced their fingers together and got them outside. It was warm and there were a few clouds, but the moon was bright and compared to the dark of the basement Amy felt like they may as well have been outside with a giant spotlight on them.

"The garage isn't far," Jo said. "We can run."

"Ok," Amy agreed weakly.

Jo kept a tight grip on Amy's hand and took a deep breath before darting off to the safety of the porch and sprinting toward the garage. Amy had no problem keeping up. She was taller than Jo by a few inches and was known for cheerleading, not for track like Jo was. For being barely five feet tall Jo was fast and they crossed the distance to the garage quickly.

Jo let go of Amy's hand so she could work the manual controls to lift the door open. With the generator dead it was the only option.

Amy stood close but had her back to Jo so she could look out towards the house for any sign of movement. She stared for a long moment at every shadow to wait for it to move or shift. Her gaze slid from spot to spot but nothing moved. Nothing seemed out of the ordinary. From the outside no one could tell there were three dead teenagers inside.

The sound of the garage door rattling and clanking made Amy jump. She spun just as she thought she'd seen something near the bushes move.

"Inside," Jo hissed and yanked her in. She didn't try to close the door which meant they had at least some light to see inside.

Amy stayed close behind her. Jo seemed to know exactly where she was going which was good. The garage, cluttered with cardboard boxes and plastic containers, surrounded the ride on mower that sat in the middle of the garage.

As Jo picked up one of the containers of gasoline and started to say something some of the moonlight coming into the garage disappeared. Amy didn't have time to turn when she hit the ground hard. She screamed as something wet and warm wrapped around her ankle.

"Amy!"

She heard but couldn't see Jo as Amy scrambled for something to grab onto but she couldn't find any purchase. The next thing she knew she was out of the garage and on the grass. Twigs poked at her and she dimly thought that was a stupid thing to be worried about when the creature was on top of her. The weight of it was so heavy she could hardly breath. She screamed, or tried to, twisting and thrashing to try and kick it off.

Somehow Amy rolled onto her back and reeled as wet, hot breath hit her in the face. The creature growled but Amy couldn't make sense of the darkness that was on top of her. It seemed like it absorbed all the light in the area and she was frantic trying to get it off her.

Pain shot through her arm and Amy felt something drip onto her face.

Off to the side Jo shouted something and then there was a splash. More liquid dripped into her face. The creature and most of the weight shifted off of Amy. Instinct took over and she rolled to the side and scrambled away on her hands and knees.

Behind her Jo shouted something again and then there was a quiet click followed by the crackling sound of fire.

There was a high-pitched screech and Amy could feel a sudden intense heat on her back. Still running on instinct Amy managed to get her feet under her and turn around.

She was nearly blinded by the towering column of fire that was just a few feet away from her. It took her a moment to realize it was the creature as it thrashed and screeched. She stared but didn't let herself hope that this would actually kill it.

Suddenly Jo was at her side. She took Amy's hand and pulled her away. The two kept staring, though, and after a moment the creature dropped to the ground and lay still. The gasoline still burned as did whatever thick cloak the creature had wrapped itself in.

"Is that it? Is it dead?" Amy managed hoarsely. She realized then that she'd gotten gasoline splashed on her when Jo had doused the creature.

"It better be," Jo said. Her voice was tight with tension but also had an edge of steel to it. Like she was daring the thing to get back up.

Amy just continued to stare for a long moment until Jo pulled her away.

"Maybe someone will notice the fire."

Amy shrugged. She brought one hand up to brush some of her loose hair from her face.

"You're bleeding!"

"What? Oh." Amy looked at the claw marks on her arm from where she'd tried to protect herself from the creature.

"We need to call the police. Or an ambulance. Or both."

"How?"

Jo didn't answer and Amy didn't push it. They made their way back to the house where they sat on the front steps and watched the creature burn. The fire had died down some but still burned bright enough to illuminate the area.

Amy wasn't sure how long they sat there. She wanted to be sure it was dead. That it wouldn't be getting up again. Jo reached over and took her hand. That made Amy look over at her.

"I'm so sorry," Jo said and she seemed to be blinking back tears.

"It's not your fault." Amy had to resist the urge to reach up and wipe her eyes. Instead she clasped Jo's hand in both of hers.

Distantly the sound of sirens could be heard, but Amy ignored it. The selfish part of her was grateful Jo was alive and sitting with her. Then she thought of Javier, the boy upstairs. The one who followed Jo around everywhere and sometimes brought her flowers between classes.

"I just wanted to have a nice weekend, I wanted to spend time with you and now..." Jo trailed off and seemed to be full on holding back tears.

Amy blinked at her in confusion. She didn't stop herself from reaching up and wiping away Jo's tears. She let her hand linger there, gently cupping her face.

Jo leaned into it.

"I'm sorry about Javier."

Jo shook her head slightly. "I invited him to let him down gently and now he's..."

Amy swallowed hard, the image of the boy's head ripped from his shoulders still fresh in her mind. He'd been the first one they found. "I'm sorry."

The sirens were getting closer and Amy looked away. Distantly she could see the lights heading their way and as relieved as she was to see them she wasn't sure how they were going to explain everything. No one was going to believe them.

The next thing she knew Jo brought a hand up to her face and turned her back to look at her. Then Jo leaned in and pressed a kiss to Amy's lips.

"Sorry," Jo apologized quickly.

Amy's brain had jammed and she stared at Jo for a moment before a faint smile appeared on her face. "It's fine. Really."

"Oh."

Amy leaned in and put an arm around Jo's shoulders. "Thank you for saving me," she said.

Jo didn't say anything. She leaned her head against Amy's shoulder. The two watched the fire as it started to die down and the first fire truck appeared at the far end of the long driveway.

ACKNOWLEDGMENTS

There is obviously a lot of behind-the-scenes work that goes into any book. There are plenty of people who helped me with this one whether they knew it or not. Luckily for me, this is the point where I get to gush about these people and how much they mean to me and the importance they had in the creation of this book.

First of all, I am eternally grateful to both my parents. Whether it was listening to my ridiculous verbal stories on long car trips or encouraging my terrible Star Wars fan-fiction you both have been incredibly patient and encouraging about my stories and my writing. I probably would have given up or gotten bored with my own writing if you hadn't insisted that I continue. Your faith in my words have given me the courage to find my voice even when I wasn't entirely sure that I wanted to.

To my longest and most constant writing companion, Casey: I hope you know how much confidence you've given me over the years. Not only have you seen my writing grow from some of my earliest days but you have gotten me to the finish line of every year of National Novel Writing Month that I have actually completed. I am still completely honored that you continue to choose to write with me after all these years. And that isn't even touching upon what an amazing friend and roommate you are to me. I don't know how I got fortunate enough to have you in my life but hopefully that continues long into our retirement in Old Wethersfield.

I also owe a huge thanks to my other roommate Marina. Our many nights watching various seasons of Pokemon and chats about writing or life in general always make me feel better. It's also always a blast getting to play the Name Game with you and Casey.

My zombie fighting partner Bri: I have such great memories of our zombie fighting. Those adventures were some of my earliest original fiction inspiration and I'm so excited to continue to collaborate with you. Your encouragement has been wonderful and you are such an inspiration to me. Your creative energy is infectious and has kept me writing even on days when doing simple things seemed like an insurmountable task.

I can't have an acknowledgements page without mentioning the person I've been friends with for nearly my entire life. Alicia, I don't know what I would do without your enthusiasm and sheer contagious energy. Our period of storytelling, however brief, is something I still hold dear to my heart and I hope to one day do justice to the stories we imagined.

Finally, thank you to anyone and everyone who has ever read anything I've created. The feedback I still occasionally receive from old fan-fiction never ceases to amaze me and has nudged me to keep going when I was sure the well of words in my head had dried up. I'm incredibly lucky to have received all the support that I have with my writing and I'll never forget it.

Lindley Valcarcel
North Andover, MA
October 2018

ABOUT THE AUTHOR

Lindley Valcarcel was born and raised on Long Island, NY and is patiently waiting for an actually scary version of *The Amityville Horror* to be created. In the meantime, she enjoys writing science fiction and horror of her own and firmly believes *The Exorcist* to be the best horror movie in existence. Should you wish to debate her on this you can find her at https://colibriwishes.wordpress.com.

This is Lindley's first book.

Join Lindley on Patreon at https://www.patreon.com/linvalcarcel. Read her blog posts weeks before everyone else and, depending on your Patreon level, read short stories that will appear in her future collections. Let her know what you think!

ALSO BY LINDLEY VALCARCEL

13, Volume 1, Supernatural Science Fiction and Horror

CONNECT WITH LINDLEY

Follow me on Bookbub:
https://www.bookbub.com/profile/Lindley-Valcarcel

Follow me on GoodReads:
https://www.goodreads.com/LindleyValcarcel

On Patreon: https://www.patreon.com/linvalcarcel. Read her blog
posts weeks before everyone else and, depending on your Patreon
level, read short stories that will appear in her future collections. Let
her know what you think!

Read my blog: https://colibriwishes.wordpress.com

Visit the Unlikely Experiments web site:
https://www.unlikely-experiments.com

www.ingramcontent.com/pod-product-compliance
Lightning Source LLC
Chambersburg PA
CBHW032041180726
48284CB00008B/2702